SHEAR MAGIC

SILVER HOLLOW PARANORMAL COZY MYSTERY SERIES BOOK 5

LEIGHANN DOBBS

TRACI DOUGLASS

SUMMARY

When wizard detective Eric Naill is found stabbed to death behind the salon of hunky witch hair stylist Graeme "Gray" Quinn, it doesn't bode well for the Quinn clan. Especially when Gray's favorite golden shears appear to be the murder weapon.

With both the Council of Wizards and the police after him, Gray must prove his innocence before he and his cousins lose everything. But when his investigation reveals a link between Eric's death and a decades-old secret, things get complicated. The only way to get to the bottom of it is to seek the help of the one woman Gray is forbidden to get close to — Starla Knight.

Meeting with Starla could spark a feud that might change Silver Hollow forever. Only it's Gray's heart that may be the worst casualty.

CHAPTER 1

Graeme "Gray" Quinn paused at the door of his hair salon, Shear Magic. His cockatoo familiar, Cosmo, repositioned himself on Gray's shoulder, flapping his wings for balance.

Something wasn't quite right.

Gray scanned the interior through the glass door. Everything looked to be in place, the chairs all facing the mirrors, razors and scissors lined up, hair products all —

"Yoo-hoo! Graeme!"

He turned to see one of his clients, Mrs. Newcastle, barreling down the sidewalk toward him. She was nearly eighty, though she looked at least ten years younger thanks to Gray's magical haircuts. She was dressed today in a pretty pastel-pink flowered dress with matching shoes. Her pink bag swung back and forth on her arm as she hurried in his direction, a look of determination on her face.

Gray plastered a smile on his face, but his shoulders slumped slightly, causing Cosmo to reposition again, this time digging his claws into Gray's thick shoulder muscles. So much for coming in early to get the shop organized before his first scheduled client.

"Good morning, Mrs. Newcastle," Gray said as she approached. "Don't you look positively radiant?"

Cosmo squawked as if in agreement.

"Oh, well. Thank you." Mrs. Newcastle patted her hair. "I'm so sorry to just drop by like this, Gray, knowing your already-packed schedule, but I have a bit of an emergency. My granddaughter is getting married this weekend, and I forgot to schedule a style and set with you. I know it's late notice, but is there any way you could fit me in?"

Professional smile firmly in place, Gray unlocked the door and poked his head inside to make sure the coast was clear and assure himself that his earlier feelings of trepidation weren't due to sensing an evil gnome or elf lying in wait. His senses told him the shop was completely empty, so he ushered her inside. He'd always been a sucker for older ladies in distress, and today was no exception. Cosmo flew to his perch in the corner while Gray gestured for Mrs. Newcastle to have a seat at his station.

Of course, working her in meant his plans to get

things done around the shop this morning were shot, but he saw no other option. At this point he'd be lucky to get his set-up done before his regular clients showed up. Still, he couldn't bring himself to turn her away. She needed his help and he'd give it. All the Quinn cousins were like that, probably because they were so close. Their families had moved to Silver Hollow a few decades ago because it was a haven for paranormal types. Life here was smooth, easy, and enjoyable — at least when they weren't investigating magical murders.

And those seemed to be occurring more frequently lately.

After removing his jacket and tugging on his black work smock, Gray quickly shampooed Mrs. Newcastle and then set about cutting her hair. About a year ago, she'd decided to change from a curly bouffant to a sleeker, pixie-cut style. It suited her elfin features well, but then again, any cut Gray would have given her would suit. That was his strongest power. With the help of his magical shears, he was able to cast beauty charms on his clients and transform them into the glorious creatures of their dreams. Because of said charms, he was by far the most successful hairdresser in town, booked solid for months in advance.

It was funny. In his teens, his three female cousins had each been so sure of their gifts, knowing exactly what their futures held. Issy had always been able to read animal minds, and at times, humans, too. She'd always said that humans were harder because there was too much clutter in their heads. Animals were clear and true. She'd always loved to hang out with animals more than people — her cousins excluded — so it was natural she'd open a pet store.

Raine had always had an extraordinary green thumb. Plants just seemed to flourish whenever she walked into a room, so of course, she'd gone into horticulture. And Ember, she'd been making delicious desserts since she'd learned to walk, so her chocolate shop was a natural extension.

Gray's future, though, hadn't been so cut and dried. In high school, he'd looked much the same as he did today — tall, dark, well muscled — except for the shamrock tattoo on his right biceps for good luck.

Flirting and dating had never been a problem for him, and he'd actually done his first haircut as a dare. One of his girlfriends had a minor hair emergency one weekend before her sister's wedding, and her usual stylist hadn't been available. Gray had always cut his own hair and done a decent job of it, so he offered to help. The girlfriend reluctantly agreed, and a legend had been born.

After graduation, he'd flown to Europe for a few months to train with an excellent stylist in Paris who also happened to be a wizard. He returned home to Silver Hollow with a whole new bag of tricks and his golden scissors in hand. These days he cut hair because he loved to do it. It was art. And he enjoyed transforming women and making their dreams come true. He loved what he did and loved working with his clients.

As he snipped and measured, his mind wandered back to all the tasks he still needed to get on top of to make sure the day ran smoothly. Looked like he'd have to hustle after he finished with Mrs. Newcastle to get it all done. He sighed. At least he didn't have to worry about carrying on a conversation this early in the morning, not with the way she chattered on about her granddaughter. Thank the goddess, given he'd not had time for coffee either.

As his client prattled on about the wedding and her other family that would be at the wedding, Gray's mind wandered. He'd lost his parents young. So had all the Quinn cousins. Perhaps that was why they were so close now. He loved each of his cousins dearly — Issy, Raine, and Ember — but lately the idea of starting a family of his own had become more and more appealing.

Too bad he'd not found anyone he wanted to settle down with, or at least anyone acceptable. Not that he didn't date or have plenty of options. A recent issue of the *Town Cryer* had named him the most eligible bachelor in Silver Hollow. His cousins teased him mercilessly over that. Gray didn't mind, but he couldn't help but wonder if someday he'd be going to the wedding of his own granddaughter. Not likely considering the way things were going.

The only girl in town who'd even come close to

capturing his heart was the one person who was strictly off limits. She belonged to the South Side witch coven, and it had been feuding with the Quinns for as long as anybody could remember. Honestly, Gray couldn't even remember what had started the row, probably some long-ago argument or snide remark, but the ill will persisted.

It had gotten to the point that the two halves of town didn't even visit the other anymore except under extraordinary circumstances. The farthest Gray had been into dreaded Southie territory had been with Issy during one of her investigations into a magical murder. They'd gone to Charmed, a small jewelry store that catered to the growing tourist crowd. It was owned by the niece of one of the South Side's most notorious wizards, Bobby Knight. Strangely, Gray didn't remember much about his visit to the store. He remembered walking in, looking around and seeing the shop's owner behind the counter, then … nothing.

Weird, that.

From his perch, Cosmo paced and squawked while staring at Gray's handiwork, as if he approved. The cawing helped bring Gray back to the present moment, and he made a mental note to give his avian friend an extra slice of orange later. Concentration was key to giving his clients the best possible results.

Mrs. Newcastle continued to chatter about how fabulous she was going to look for the wedding and how Gray always gave her the perfect cut. He'd partially finished one side of her cut, but he needed his special golden trimming shears to do the rest. He gave her a bland smile while reaching into a drawer for them.

What most of his clients didn't know was that those particular golden scissors were specially infused with magic, even more so than his other tools. Magic that helped him create the most flattering style for each hair type and face shape, depending on the client. Styles that also seemed to remove years from the client's age as well. He'd visited a special wizard barber in Switzerland to have them made and blessed just for his purposes. He'd had them for years now, and they felt like a part of him. He wasn't sure what he'd do if they were lost or damaged.

As he fumbled around in the drawer with one hand, a cat with charcoal-colored fur and orange-gold eyes trotted in through the small cat door he'd had installed in the front of the place.

Brimstone was a local familiar who hung around with the Quinns and was quite opinionated. He didn't really belong to any one of the cousins and answered to no one but served them all as needed — even if his elevated opinion of himself did leave something to be desired.

Cosmo squawked from his perch and flapped his wings, startling the feline. Brimstone skittered sideways, hissing with fright, then caught himself and shook it off, sauntering away again as if he'd planned to nearly dive under the storage cabinet.

He padded up to Gray and swished his tail. Thankfully, only witches could hear their familiars talk; otherwise poor Mrs. Newcastle might have had a coronary. As with most of his clients, she was not of the paranormal community. In fact, most of the humans they lived side by side with had no idea there were magical folk among them, sometimes living right next door.

For many years, that had been something of a taboo. No paranormal–human mixing allowed beyond the purely polite. But recently his cousin Issy had moved in with a human man she'd fallen in love with, and all seemed to be going well. Dex had accepted her powers, even if he didn't fully understand them. Gray hoped someday to make a love match like that himself, magical or otherwise.

"Looking for something?" Brimstone asked him in his usual snooty cat tone.

"My favorite shears," Gray said, without thinking, still fumbling in the drawer for his golden scissors. "I always store them in here, but ..."

"I'm sorry, dear. What did you say?" Mrs. Newcastle asked.

"Oh, nothing. I'm sorry, just talking to myself." He gave Brimstone a look over his shoulder. "I seem to have misplaced my best shears."

That really bothered Gray, because he always kept things neat and tidy in the salon and could've sworn he'd put them away in the drawer the night before. He always put them back in the drawer. No way would he have left them out to be lost or damaged or —

"Are they gold and about as long as the chew sticks Issy gives to Bella?" Brimstone asked. Bella was Issy's Pomeranian familiar. Cute as a button, even if she was still learning the ropes.

Gray nodded, the sick knot in his stomach tightening. The absence of the scissors might explain that strange feeling he'd had in front of the shop. If anything happened to those scissors ...

"I believe they're in back," Brimstone said in between grooming his paws.

Huh. That was odd, because that was where he kept all the cleaning supplies and extra smocks, brooms, and extra inventory. He'd never put the shears in the storage area with such caustic chemicals. He was the only stylist in the shop, so that ruled out another person moving them. It wasn't unheard of for a spell to go astray in Silver Hollow, so maybe that was what he'd sensed when he'd first opened up.

"Excuse me a moment, Mrs. Newcastle," Gray said, bowing slightly to hide his growing frown. "I'll be right back."

He followed Brimstone into the storage area, his expression darkening to a scowl as the cat added, "I don't think you're going to like where you find them."

That much was obvious. He searched through all the shelves and boxes but didn't find the shears anywhere.

Brimstone was no help, sitting atop the top shelf and blinking down at Gray as he rummaged through endless boxes. Finally he sighed and straightened, hands on his hips, and narrowed his gaze on the cat. "You're mistaken. They're not here."

"I never said they were in the storage room." Brimstone gave him a flat stare. "I was wondering what you were looking for."

"You said in back."

"Exactly." The cat's orange gaze flickered to the rear exit of the shop before returning to Gray. "In. The. Back."

"Oh." Now he was really confused. Did Brimstone mean they were outside? No way would he take his precious golden shears outside, where they would be exposed to the elements. The wizard had warned him the day he'd picked them up that leaving them to the rain or snow or even in high humidity would ruin them. Bile rose hot in his throat as Gray walked to the door, the tension in his gut now turning into painful cramps. The feeling that something was definitely wrong was confirmed as he touched the knob and a zing of residual magic zapped his fingertips.

Uh-oh.

Gray hesitated. Why would there be magic on the doorknob? He remembered the strange feeling of something not being right that had come over him at the front door.

He turned the knob and opened the door. Early-morning sunshine poured in, temporarily blinding him. Everything in the alley was just a dark shadow against the bright sun in his eyes. The hulking Dumpster. The trash cans behind O'Hara's Pub. The elm tree that grew next to the paper-goods store.

The body lying a few feet from Gray's door.

Oh no!

Gray rushed over to see if he could help. The man lay face down, unmoving. Was it one of the shop owners who had come to toss something in the Dumpster and fallen? A heart attack, maybe?

But as he bent down, he realized that wasn't the problem. Now that the sun wasn't directly in his eyes, he saw the details. The man, who Gray didn't recognize, was beyond help. Even before he felt his wrist for a pulse, Gray knew he was gone from this world.

The cause of his death wasn't a heart attack. No, it was something worse. Far worse — especially for Gray, because the cause of death appeared to be his golden shears, which were sticking straight out of the man's back like a deadly beacon.

STOMACH CHURNING, Gray stumbled back inside and grabbed the cordless phone from its charger in the back room. He quickly dialed 9-1-1 and reported the body. Mind racing and body oddly numb, he tried to get his thoughts in order. For a man who'd investigated plenty of murders with Issy, it was definitely different when it was your shop and livelihood that were involved. Livelihood. The shop. The last thing he needed was for Mrs. Newcastle to be here when the police arrived.

His clients liked to talk, and word of mouth accounted for a huge portion of his business. He wanted them chatting about his great cuts and skill with scissors, not dead people in his alley. He tossed the phone aside and rushed to the front to get rid of Mrs. Newcastle before the cops arrived. He didn't want her to be upset or inconvenienced by the police, and he had a sinking feeling his business would be disrupted enough as it was. Her hair was only half done, one side noticeably shorter than the other, but there was nothing to be done about it now.

"But dear," Mrs. Newcastle protested as Gray guided her toward the front door. "My hair isn't finished."

He quickly finger-styled her short spikes before putting her hat back on top of it all. "You look marvelous. The natural look is all the rage now, along with asymmetrical cuts. You'll be the envy of everyone at the wedding."

Luckily, Gray got her out the door just before the squad car pulled up, sans siren, thankfully. Owen Gleason, the police chief, and DeeDee Clawson, his deputy, got out.

Across the street, he saw his cousin Issy rushing from her shop, Enchanted Pets. Her strawberry-blond curls shined bright in the morning sun, bouncing around her like happy pennies. Her face was pinched with worry, and he shook his head in a signal that there was nothing to worry about and she should go back to her shop. He could deal with this and didn't want to interrupt her work day.

Gray still felt oddly detached, as if all this was happening to someone else. There was a dead person. Behind his shop. Where he made his living. Not only was that bad luck, it was very bad karma. He'd have to hit Raine up for some sage so he could conduct a ritual cleansing of the area, banish the dark energy, remove the bad vibes. But first he needed to tell the police what he knew, which was precious little at this point.

"What's this about a dead body?" Owen asked, walking up to Gray. As usual, he'd shunned his normal uniform in favor of a garish Hawaiian shirt and khaki pants. This one was varying shades of pinks and yellows in a sunset motif, with beach umbrellas and palm trees scattered through it. With his shaggy blond hair and flip-flops, the guy looked more like a surfer than local law enforcement. Owen leaned past Gray to peer into the shop. "Where's it at?"

"Not in there," Gray said, rapidly losing patience and composure. "Out back in the alley."

Issy rushed up to the group — apparently she'd ignored Gray's signal — and they all headed through the salon and out the back exit. Gray's legs felt shaky, and he kept having to mentally check himself to make sure he wasn't acting as strangely as he felt. He was a big guy, six foot plus, and wasn't prone to passing out, but the shock of finding the body and his lack of food and caffeine this morning were getting to him.

Cosmo was going nuts on his perch, flapping and squawking, prancing back and forth and bobbing his plumed head. DeeDee stopped to scratch his head on her way through and gave Gray a concerned glance. She was paranormal too, a werewolf shifter, and usually did her best to steer the all-human Owen away from any evidence that might incriminate their kind. They preferred to handle paranormal trouble within their own community. Gray was used to assisting on those investigations, not being the center of one himself. He definitely liked being on the other side of things better. He stepped out the back door and stopped next to DeeDee. They'd been good friends for years, and he was glad to have her support.

In the alleyway, Owen walked carefully around the body, then crouched to examine it. After pulling on a pair of latex gloves, he gingerly turned the corpse over to identify the victim.

Issy gasped.

DeeDee hissed.

Gray felt a jolt of surprise run through him. He hadn't recognized the victim before because he didn't know him very well, but now that he could see his face, he realized it was Eric Naill, a local wizard and private detective. But why would he have been at Gray's shop, snooping in the alley?

"Interesting ..." Owen pressed his lips together and glanced up at Gray. "It's Eric Naill. I wonder what he was doing out here."

"I have no idea." Gray turned away, his broad shoulders slumping. Whatever Eric had been doing back here, this was not good at all. Normal deaths were bad enough in this town. A wizard death was very serious business among the paranormals living in Silver Hollow, and finding a dead one in back of Gray's salon, with his golden scissors protruding from it, didn't bode well for him, his business, or the Quinn clan.

CHAPTER 2

For the next hour or so, Owen and DeeDee, along with several new deputies they'd recently hired to help around the station, continued to process the crime scene. Owen had no idea about the magical part of his community. The Quinns and especially DeeDee did their best to keep him from finding out about their kind. In fact, DeeDee was tossing out any scenario she could come up with that didn't involve witches and spells and curses to try to throw Owen off the track.

"Maybe it was some cult thing. You know how they like to congregate in the mountains around these parts." DeeDee straightened and narrowed her gaze on the body. "Maybe even some rock band or something, with that long hair. Drugs, perhaps. Professional rivalry."

"Naill was a private detective. Worked with him on a

couple of cases this past year," Owen said, staring down at the body. He didn't seem inclined to buy any of DeeDee's wild theories today. Just Gray's luck. "Nice enough guy, bit secretive though, for my tastes. Guess you'd have to be in his line of work, though. Always sneaking around, trying to get evidence, trying to catch people doing things they shouldn't."

DeeDee gave Gray a wary glance. Owen had no idea the victim was also a wizard.

"What about these fancy scissors?" Owen asked, glancing up at Gray. "They belong to you, Graeme?"

Uh oh. He was using Gray's full name now, never a good sign.

"Yes." Gray swallowed hard, doing his best not to stare at his magical shears sticking out of the man's back. They'd be useless now.

He'd have to order another pair from the wizard in Switzerland, if they'd even allow him to have another pair. Craftsmen like that wizard took their implements seriously and expected others to do so. Gray had had to undergo a stringent background check when he'd ordered a pair.

This time he wasn't sure he'd pass muster, given that the first pair had ended up embedded in someone's spinal cord. Of course, he'd had nothing to do with that and no idea how they'd gotten out here, but still. He'd need answers, and good ones, if he hoped to ever get another pair of magical golden scissors. He exhaled slowly and did his best to keep his voice steady. "I noticed them missing this morning when I was working on Mrs. Newcastle. That's what brought me out here, and I found him."

"Huh." Owen gave DeeDee a look, his expression considering. "You just noticed they were gone this morning. Was there any sign of a break-in when you arrived today? Locks tampered with? A broken window maybe?"

"No, I don't think so. I was in kind of a rush because Mrs. Newcastle showed up unexpectedly. She wasn't on my regular schedule today, but I was doing her a favor by working her in. As far as I remember, the front door was closed and locked as usual, and there was nothing missing or out of place in the storeroom. No broken windows either."

Owen walked past Gray to inspect the rear door of the salon. "Well, there's no evidence of tampering with the lock here either or signs of a break-in. How do you imagine the killer got your scissors, Gray? Not like most people would think to use some fancy cutting scissors from a hair salon to kill someone, right? You got any enemies, people who'd like to see you taken down a peg or two?"

"No idea." Sure, he'd had minor disagreements with people over the years, but nothing major and certainly nothing that would warrant murder. He barely knew Eric Naill and had no reason to want to harm him. And as for who would take his scissors, he had no clue. The Quinns were generally well liked in the community except by those who were up to no good. He ran through the list of people he'd helped Issy investigate — the Vonners, the Pettywoods, DeeDee's new husband, Caine Hunter — but none of them seemed likely suspects. Christian Vonner was imprisoned. Enid Pettywood and her niece were back on solid footing with the magical community. And Caine and DeeDee were blissfully happy together, and he was deep into production on his next horror movie, *Revenge of the Living Bloodsuckers 4*.

Caine had come to Silver Hollow to produce vampire, werewolf, and monster movies. What better place to do that than in a town of paranormals? It worked out quite well, because the residents thought nothing of seeing fur, fangs, and dark cloaks around town.

Ursula Lavoie, the medical examiner, glanced up and met Gray's gaze from beneath her enormous gray hoodie. She was a real vampire, not the foolish, imaginary kind in Caine's campy horror flicks, and part of the paranormal community here in Silver Hollow. From the victim's identity and the trace magic still pulsing off those golden shears, she'd know this was a paranormal killing. Her attention darted from Gray to DeeDee and then back again before she stood and ordered her assistants to pack up the body. "I'll let you know as soon as I find anything, Owen."

"And I can take witness statements, boss," DeeDee chimed in, volunteering in hopes of keeping the paranormal aspect of this hush-hush from the humans, Gray was sure. He appreciated her efforts, even if he wouldn't have much to tell her. "See if anyone saw anything. I'll walk back to headquarters when I'm done. Nice enough day for it."

"Fine." Owen raked a hand through his tousled blond hair, giving an aggrieved sigh. "I need to get back to the station for a meeting. More paperwork and regulations. Call me after you talk to people, Deputy."

"Will do." DeeDee waited until Owen was gone before turning back to Gray with a frown. "This doesn't look good for you, buddy. Eric was found behind your shop with your scissors sticking out of his back. Now, I know you didn't do this and you know you didn't do this. But Owen? Not so much. Best tell me exactly what you can about all this so I've got something to go on."

That was the problem, though. He knew squat about what had happened here. And yes, he and DeeDee had been good friends for years. They had a special bond, but he knew that friendship would go only so far.

"I would if I could," Gray said, shaking his head. "But I swear I have no idea how this happened or why. You know what I know. I came in earlier this morning to get some paperwork and things done around the shop, but when I arrived, Mrs. Newcastle was waiting by the front door, just like I told Owen. She said she'd forgotten to book an appointment before her granddaughter's wedding this weekend and begged me to work her in.

You know I'm a sucker for old ladies in distress, so I didn't refuse."

DeeDee rolled her eyes and snorted, jotting his statement in her trusty notebook. Mrs. Newcastle's memory wasn't the greatest these days. She'd called the police a week or so ago, from what DeeDee had told Gray, to report her best china missing, only to later find it in her pantry, right where it belonged.

"I was rushing then, to get her done before my regular clients started showing up, so I never had a chance to check the back room like I usually do. I just got started working on her. Then Brimstone showed up while I was fumbling for my scissors in the drawer, and he told me to check out back. That's when I found Eric's body."

Cosmo swooped through the still-open back door to sit on Gray's shoulder and nuzzle his neck with his head and beak, offering what comfort and support he could. Gray appreciated it more than he could say. Witches' familiars were more than magical helpers. They were close confidants and friends, members of the family.

"Don't try to blame this on me. I was just reporting what I saw." Brimstone paced around where the body had been, sniffing. "I smell a paranormal's scent."

Issy crouched near the area then turned to squint at the lock on the back door and sniffed. "Smells like wax. I'd bet good money someone tried to use magic to pick the lock."

They all stood and stared down at the chalk outline

where Eric Naill's corpse had been. Gray sighed. "Why would Eric break into my salon? He was a wizard, so if he wanted a lock open, he'd open it. No 'try' about it. If he'd come here to get inside my shop, then someone must have stopped him before he could finish. But who?"

"Good question," Issy said. "Maybe someone else was breaking into your shop and Eric surprised him."

"And *that* person killed him," DeeDee said, finishing her notes before closing her notebook and shoving it into the pocket of her navy-blue uniform pants. "But the question still remains: What was the killer looking for, and did he or she find it here at Gray's shop?"

CHAPTER 3

With his salon now a crime scene, Gray had no choice but to close up shop for the day. Just the thought of all the lost revenue and damage to his business reputation nearly gutted him. He'd worked hard over the years to make Shear Magic the salon to visit in Silver Hollow. Now, with one fell swoop, it was all gone.

Could that have been a motive? Did someone hate him enough to want to ruin his business? But who? And why? Thinking about it gave him a headache. He generally tried to get along with everyone and had precious little time to walk on the wild side or anywhere else in his free hours. Most of the time, when he wasn't working, he was at home working on his cabin or with his cousins.

Not exactly a rip-roaring, excitement-filled life, but it was good enough for him.

Reluctantly, he called all his clients for the next few days and rearranged their appointments, then gathered Cosmo from his perch, locked the place, and then walked a few blocks to meet Issy and his other cousins at the Main Squeeze juice bar. It had opened a year ago during the whole natural-food craze sweeping the country. Karen Dixon, the owner, did a brisk business year round.

The walk did him good. He needed some fresh air to clear his head after the horror of finding Eric's body. Plus he was glad to get away from the shop for a bit. He hoped to talk to Luigi Romano. Luigi, a wizard in their paranormal community, ran the pizza shop attached to the juice bar. Maybe he'd heard something about who might want to kill Eric Naill with Gray's shears. The wizards in Silver Hollow were a tight bunch and held regular meetings. Surely somebody in their group would know something.

When he arrived, the gang was all there. His cousin Ember looked fresh as a spring daisy in her sunny yellow sundress, her long, dark auburn hair spilling down her back. She ran the local candy shop, Divine Cravings, and was as sweet as the confections she sold. Raine, his other cousin, sat slumped in her chair across the table from him. She still appeared to be a bit depressed after her run-in with a demon last year. They'd been trying to help solve a murder case, and she'd been inadvertently possessed. It could take a while for the lingering effects to wear off. Thankfully, her greenhouse business, Green Goddess Landscaping and Florist, kept her busy. She wore her usual work uniform of green overalls over a white T-shirt, and her stick-straight copper hair was plaited into braids on either side of her head. She had a blue bandana tied around her forehead, and dirt streaked her forearms. She often claimed she could read plant minds, though she kept that pretty quiet because most people didn't believe that plants had minds.

The place was packed, despite the nip of chill still in the air. They'd been lucky to get a table on the patio. Birds chirped, and the scent of freshly mown grass filled the air. At least the sun beaming down kept it from being too cold. Gray took a seat at the round wrought iron table and leaned back so Cosmo could step off onto the back of his chair.

"I'm so sorry to hear about what happened this morning, Gray," Ember said, reaching into the basket at her feet to pull out Bellatrix and Endora, her two kitten familiars. The fuzzy balls of black and white fur never seemed to get any older or bigger. "How terrible that must have been to walk out and find that behind your shop."

Cosmo squawked from near Gray's shoulder.

"Got that right, buddy," he said, scratching the cockatoo's head. "No. It wasn't a pleasant way to start the day, that's for sure." Gray sighed and sank further into his seat. "I can't figure out why he's dead or who would do it. And why they choose my place as the scene of the crime. The best I can figure is that the murder must have had something to do with one of Eric's cases."

"Maybe someone had a vendetta against him?" Issy suggested, setting her Pomeranian familiar, Bella, on her lap. The fluffy little marmalade-colored dog turned in a circle three times before settling right where she'd started. "We scented magic and a paranormal at the scene, but I suppose it could have been a human, perhaps in cahoots with someone in our community. Did you know someone who'd hired him for a case, Gray? Or had he come around to question you recently?"

"No. That's the thing. I had literally no contact with the guy at all prior to —"

Luigi waved to Gray from the window of his pizza shop and gestured for them to come over, severing Gray's response. Their group walked inside the small restaurant, the delicious smells of baked cheese and garlic wafting around them, and took a seat at the table Luigi indicated.

"I heard about Eric's murder," Luigi said once they'd been seated away from the other customers. He was a big guy, tall and stout, with frizzy shoulder-length brown hair and a long, scruffy dark beard down to his mid-chest. He wore a duster as if he'd just walked off some sci-fi western film. Not exactly a man who avoided attention.

Luigi had been sent to Silver Hollow a while back by

"the committee" — the regional group of witches and wizards that oversaw the various communities and made sure the paranormals didn't get too out of hand. It wouldn't do to have "normals" figure out that there were beings with special gifts living among them. He also made sure no one used dark magic — magic that might harm another.

Because it was Luigi's job to keep an eye on the local paranormal community, the magical folk were still a bit wary of him. Gray was warming to him, though. He thought the guy was more interested in making pizza than giving names to the committee for punishment, and he seemed likable enough. Plus, he'd never turned anyone in even though he'd had plenty of chances.

"What did the cops find out? Anything yet?" Luigi asked.

"Not yet," Gray said, shaking his head. "And I need some answers soon before my business reputation is permanently marred by this. We're thinking maybe the death had something to do with one of the cases Eric was working on. Do you know what he was investigating?"

"Hmm, let me think." Luigi took the open seat at their table, his expression pensive as he toyed with his beard. "Last time I talked to him, he mentioned doing something for Timothy Stevens."

"Oh, like what?" Issy asked. "Tim is such a nice guy, I can't imagine why he'd need a PI."

"I don't know the details, but there was some kind of

scandal surrounding Tim's father a long time ago," Luigi said.

"Scandal?" Issy asked. "I thought his father died."

Luigi nodded solemnly. "You Quinns probably wouldn't remember because it happened when you were just kids. Tim's father was apparently involved in something about thirty years ago, right before he died. You know that was by his own hand, right? Yeah, nasty business that. Anyway, rumors were that it had something to do with the South Side witches. That was during a time when rules about Northies and Southies hanging together were a bit more lax, but anything too serious like a relationship or business deal was frowned upon." Luigi shook his head and shrugged. "Don't know why Tim would hire Eric now, after all these years. I wouldn't think he'd want anything about his father dug up."

South Side witches? Did Eric's death have something to do with the South Side witches? That would not be good. Not good at all. Investigating a Southie would be nearly impossible for Gray.

For as long as Gray could remember, it had been a rule that they should avoid Southies at all costs. That had been a problem when they were in high school, because Silver Hollow only had one high school. They'd had to attend with South Side kids. Of course they'd always steered clear of each other. Well, at least *most* of the time.

"So, Tim's father was a wizard?" Ember asked,

cuddling a kitten beneath her chin while the other fussed and tried to take its place. "Is Tim one too?"

"Nah, Tim's no wizard. Not that I know of, anyway. He's nonmagical like his mother," Luigi said. "But his father was pretty powerful, at least according to Martin Ellsworth. He investigated everything back then. The father apparently hid his abilities from both his son and his wife."

"Yikes." Issy sat back in her seat. "I never imagined Tim would have any kind of scandal in his background. He's a customer at my shop. I sold him a saltwater aquarium a while back. He comes in periodically for new fish and supplies. Always so pleasant and polite."

"I know him too," Ember said. "He comes into Divine Cravings a lot. Tim's mother likes my vanilla creams. She's homebound now, and he takes care of her. And he likes the peppermint bark."

"Yeah, Tim probably doesn't even know about what happened back then. Probably nothing to do with what happened to Eric. You know, now that I think about it," Luigi scratched his jaw, "I remember Eric telling me about a run-in he had with Beth Wilkins recently."

Gray's spirits fell further. Beth Wilkins was a middle-aged witch known around Silver Hollow for being a little crazy. Her memory was shot, and she couldn't perform magic any longer. Every time Gray had seen her, she'd been rambling on about the good old days. So sad and so very unhelpful for his current situation. He needed answers, not mad ramblings.

"Was it at O'Hara's Pub?" he asked Luigi. "I hear that's where she spends most of her time these days, especially now that she can't work at the applesauce factory."

"Not sure," Luigi said. "Eric only said they'd argued. Don't know about what, but I think Martin's keeping an eye on her now that her condition seems to be worsening."

From where they sat in the corner, Gray could hear the conversation at the next table over. Two older women were discussing Mrs. Newcastle's hair. He bit back a sad chuckle as one of the ladies said she thought it looked ridiculous. The other agreed but pointed out that Mrs. Newcastle said it was one of the latest styles. Great. Not only was his shop closed, people were talking about his latest haircut, and not in a complimentary manner. This couldn't be good for business.

"I'm too old for the latest styles," one lady said.

"I don't know," the second said. "Fanny Newcastle looked much younger with that cut. Maybe I should consider making an appointment."

Okay, maybe not so bad if one of them was still considering an appointment.

"Speaking of Martin Ellsworth," Luigi said, drawing Gray's attention back to his own table. "He seemed to think it was mighty suspicious Eric was found outside

Shear Magic, with your golden shears in his back. You might want to watch yourself for the time being, friend. There appears to be trouble headed your way."

From where Gray was sitting, trouble had already set up shop and hung out a welcome sign. He watched as Luigi went back into the kitchen to help prep for the lunch rush. An ominous silence fell over the group. Gray couldn't blame his cousins for the awkwardness. Considering a dead body had been found on his premises, he wouldn't know what to say either.

Things like this seemed to follow the Quinns around like a loyal puppy. But sitting here, feeling sorry for himself, wasn't getting him anywhere. He needed to take action and investigate the death himself as soon as possible. Things weren't looking good for him at present on either side of the fence — human or paranormal. Owen seemed as suspicious as Luigi, and he fully expected to be hauled into the police station for questioning soon.

Issy patted Gray's arm. "Don't worry, cuz, we're not going to let you take the fall for this."

"That's right. We'll investigate it ourselves," Raine added with an unlikely burst of enthusiasm.

"I think we should start by talking with Tim Stevens and Beth Wilkins," Issy added.

"But what if what Luigi said was true?" Ember asked. "If his father was a wizard and this murder has something to do with the South Side witches, then how in the world will we ever investigate that?"

CHAPTER 4

While Issy, Raine and Ember headed back to their shops, Gray felt a bit discombobulated. He couldn't go back to Shear Magic because the police were still investigating, so he sat at the juice bar table alone, feeling a bit gloomy. He had managed to send off a message to the maker of the magic shears in Switzerland, doing his best to explain what had happened and why he needed a replacement pair. So far, he'd not received a response. All the stress was getting to him. He normally worked out his problems while he cut a client's hair. The precision of snipping strands to form a cohesive whole helped center him and clear his head, making it easier to find a solution to whatever issue he faced. Now, though, when he needed that clarity most, it was elusive. Deep in his heart, he feared he might never get it back.

Brimstone walked up and sat near his ankle. "Told you things didn't look good."

"Thanks for the reminder," Gray muttered. Hearing those words did not help make him feel better. "So far I haven't heard anything from DeeDee about the police investigation, and I have no idea how we're supposed to look into any of this ourselves."

"Yeah, I heard the part about the South Side witches." Brimstone purred low. "Maybe I can help. There's a certain tabby familiar over there I sometimes associate with."

"Really?" Gray patted the seat of the chair beside him, and Brimstone hopped up. "Isn't that considered walking on the wild side?"

"I can obviously go places humans can't. And your petty human rules don't apply to me," the cat said in a superior feline tone. "Given my stature in the local familiar community, no one questions if I take a jaunt over to the South Side of Silver Hollow to check things out." Brimstone swished his tail, preening. "A sleek ginger tiger cat there and I have developed a certain … rapport."

Cosmo squawked and bobbed his head, speaking telepathically to Gray. "I can help too. I can fly over the area and scope things out, boss."

Gray scratched the bird's head and smiled. "Thanks for the offers, both of you, but we don't even know for sure if the South Side coven is involved in any of this yet, though my instincts tell me that's a definite possibility. But given what Luigi said, maybe it was crazy old Beth who did Eric in. Or Tim Stevens, as unlikely as that sounds. Probably best not to send either of you on a wild goose chase until we have more to go on. Besides, Issy and I are going to Tim's house later to talk with him. I'll know more after that."

"Fine, have it your way." Brimstone jumped down off the chair and strutted away. "See you later."

Gray watched the cat go then got up and walked to his car, the South Side coven still stuck in his mind — or rather, one witch in particular.

As he drove past the small strip of forest that divided Silver Hollow into north and south sections, images of Starla Knight flitted through his mind. Back in high school, she'd been all long blond curls and deep midnight-blue eyes. He'd found her intoxicating, intriguing, forbidden fruit.

He'd never acted on any of that, of course. It just wasn't done. And now, with all the rumors of hexes and curses flying around for anyone from the north who dared set foot in the south, it would be crazy to set foot on the South Side again. Still, he was desperate and his options were dwindling by the hour, so perhaps he'd take a chance after all. This wooded area was considered a neutral zone, where magical folk from either side of town could meet and conduct business, because crossing over into another coven's territory without invitation was frowned upon. As long as he stayed within its boundaries, he was fine.

Unfortunately, with his mind otherwise occupied, Gray drove right past the forest and straight into the South Side coven's territory. Before he knew what he was doing, he was driving by a jewelry shop called Charmed, owned by the woman foremost in his mind.

He parked his black SUV near the curb and cut the engine, watching the storefront as tourists came and went. It looked much the same as it had the last time he'd been here with Issy. Same quaint stone-cottage exterior, same glittering interior filled with all sorts of charms and jewels and crystals for any occasion. Through the front window, he spotted Starla behind the register, smiling at a customer she waited on, still just as pretty and puzzling as ever. She'd never given him any indication she even noticed him beyond the usual hello and goodbye, which was odd, because he was a guy who was used to standing out.

Exhaling slowly, he turned the key and restarted the engine. This was getting him exactly nowhere, and the sooner he got back on his own side of town, the better. Then Starla glanced in his direction, her deep-blue eyes locking with his across the distance, and once more he was enthralled. A strange, silent connection seemed to sizzle between them, same as it had long ago when he and Issy had gone into the store to question her. Then, as fast as it had started, Starla looked away, and the connection was broken.

Gray found himself breathing fast and deep, hands gripped tight on the steering wheel, doing his best to keep it together. It was ridiculous. It was dangerous. It was delightful.

He glanced back again. Starla was still busy with the customer, but the orange tabby Brimstone had spoken about crouched on the front step, her striped tail curled around her, golden-orange eyes watching him.

For the first time since this whole mess started, he felt a wee bit of hope.

Starla had helped the Quinns on a case once before. He wondered if she might again.

If the South Side coven was somehow involved in this, she would be their best bet in finding out. Her uncle, Bobby Knight, had been one of the most notorious wizards in their coven. He was known to be a hothead and a cheat, among other, less kind things. Though he hadn't heard much about Bobby lately — the guy was middle-aged, so maybe he'd slowed down — he couldn't help but feel this might involve him. That meant one thing: Gray needed to talk to Starla.

Realizing he'd been sitting there longer than was prudent, Gray quickly drove off, back toward the north side of town. It wouldn't look good to get caught where he shouldn't be right now, and he didn't want to be late for his meeting with Issy. The last thing he needed right now was for someone to see him coming from the south and start asking questions about why he'd been there. He had enough trouble on his hands as it was. Later, he'd ask Brimstone to help him arrange a meeting with Starla in the woods to see if he could get her cooperation in his investigation.

Until then, he needed to concentrate on his upcoming meeting with Tim Stevens.

CHAPTER 5

Issy and Gray walked up to Tim Stevens's doorstep later that afternoon. They were there under the guise of bringing a special delivery of saltwater fish food for him from the new shipment Issy had received earlier that day. Gray knocked on the door and then stepped back.

Moments later, Tim answered, looking a bit worse for wear. Then again, Ember had mentioned him being caretaker for his mother, who had dementia — a hard job that would leave anyone a bit frazzled at times. Tim was around thirty, the same age as the Quinns, though the dark circles under his eyes and strain of dealing with his sick mother made him look a bit older. His clothes were a bit cockeyed, and one of his shoes was unlaced. Issy gave Gray a look, clearly feeling bad for showing up unannounced, but they had to find out what Tim knew before things turned any worse for Gray.

"Hi, Tim," Issy said brightly. "Sorry for the surprise call, but I got some new fish food in the shop today and thought you might like to try some." She held up the bag in her hand. "May we come in for a second? Gray is thinking of getting a tank himself, and I wanted to show him your setup."

"Oh, well." Tim glanced back into his tiny house, then shoved his glasses further up his nose. His dark hair looked slightly rumpled, as if he'd been running his hands through it. "Uh, I guess it would be all right. Mom's taking a nap, so you'll have to be quiet, though."

"No problem. Thanks for letting us take a look." Issy walked inside, followed by Gray. She handed Tim the bag before walking over to the fish tank along the wall. Gray flashed what he hoped was a friendly smile, despite the awkwardness of the moment.

The house was clean, if dated, all the furnishings looking like they came from the seventies at the latest. Lots of burnt orange and mustard yellows. The shag carpeting was a nondescript brown, and the walls were beige. Gray took a deep breath, scenting coffee, bacon, and a combination of mothballs and mustiness. It didn't seem Tim or his mother got out much. Given that she was incoherent most of the time and her son might be a murderer, Gray understood why.

"Such a shame about Eric Naill, eh?" Issy said,

straightening from where she'd crouched to peer inside the aquarium. The tank was the only bright spot in the otherwise dim room. Brightly lit from behind, neon-hued fish swam slowly through the turquoise water. Green plants swayed in the bubbles and currents, and pristine white sand sparkled from the floor of the aquarium. Whatever Tim's other faults might be, he took excellent care of his fish.

"What do you mean?" Tim's expression was guarded.

"Found dead this morning in the alley behind my shop," Gray said, taking over for Issy. The words still stuck in his throat, but he forced them out, doing his best to keep his voice steady. "Stabbed in the back. Police are still searching for suspects."

"Dead?" Tim stumbled over a side table and slumped into a threadbare recliner.

Not exactly the reaction Gray had expected, especially if Tim was the one who'd done the deed. Yes, the news was upsetting, but as far as he knew, Tim and Eric hadn't been that close. Was he acting at being surprised? Issy rushed over to pat a distraught Tim on the back.

"You seem really upset," Gray said.

"Well, a man *is* dead. That's upsetting."

"Could there be another reason?"

Tim's eyes narrowed. "What's that supposed to mean?"

"Like maybe he was working for you and now the answers to whatever you had him doing died with him."

Gray's words earned him a stern look from Issy. He hadn't meant to be so blunt, but considering he was suspect number one on law enforcement's list, any subtlety Gray possessed had gone right out the window. He gentled his tone a bit and continued. "Is that true, Tim? Did you hire Eric?"

A babbling female voice came from down the hall, where Gray assumed Tim's mother was asleep in the bedroom — or was supposed to be. He heard the words "toads" and "shaving cream" distinctly. Gray and Issy exchanged a look.

Tim glanced nervously in the direction of the voice. "Where did you hear that?"

Gray studied the other man. He could hit him with a truth spell or reach into his mind with a reading hex, but that sort of witchcraft was frowned upon. Besides, Tim looked like he would cave pretty easily without any sorcery.

"Around town. If it's true, you might as well tell us. It will all come out in the investigation," Gray said.

"Investigation?" Tim cast another worried glance in the direction of the bedrooms. Was he worried his mother might wake up or worried about an investigation?

"Into his murder," Gray added. "Naturally they'll be looking into his clients first."

Tim looked at Gray uncertainly as he pushed up from the recliner. "That's supposed to be confidential."

"Not in a murder investigation it won't be."

Tim glanced down the hallway again and sighed. "Hold on."

He went down the hall, and Gray heard a door close. Then Tim came back and plopped in the recliner again.

"Sorry, I don't want Mom to overhear this and get upset." Tim fiddled with his glasses again then leaned forward with his forearms on his thighs. "She wasn't always like this, you know. She used to be like a normal mom. But over the years, she's gotten worse and worse. Aunt Sadie said she was fine until Dad's accident." Tim's voice broke and he looked down at his feet.

Accident? Gray would've sworn Luigi said Tim's father took his own life. Then again, it had been a long time ago, and Tim would've been a child. Maybe in the aftermath of it all, Tim's mother had lied about how his father died to protect him from the truth.

Gray felt a pang of guilt. Poor guy was just trying to protect his mother, and here Gray was interrogating him and practically accusing him of being a murderer.

"So why did you hire Eric?" Gray's voice was more gentle this time.

Tim sniffed, still looking at his feet. "I just want Mom to have some peace. I'd do *anything* for her. But her care is getting harder and harder. And more expensive. The insurance company dismissed some claims that I recently filed on her behalf, and I wanted to make sure I had my facts straight before I took the company to court. That's why I hired Eric. He's looking into some of the insurance rules and legalities for me. You know, making sure the insurance company doesn't screw me over." He looked back up at them and shrugged. "I had no problem with Eric at all, I swear. I didn't kill him. Why would I when he was helping me?"

Gray glanced at Issy, and she nodded. He got the impression that Tim was telling the truth. Plus, he highly doubted the guy had it in him to commit murder. Then again, people can do extraordinary things when motivated. But it seemed Tim's whole world was his mother, and because he was depending on Eric to help him with the insurance claim, he certainly wouldn't want the guy dead.

Despite the ruse being up, Gray spent a few minutes oohing and aahing over Tim's aquarium. It really was nice, and he even asked Tim a few questions about the fish and upkeep. Finally it was time for him and Issy to go. No more sounds came from the room at the end of the hall.

"Thanks so much for speaking to us, Tim," Issy said at the door. "I can't imagine how hard it must be for you, caring for your mother alone like this. If you ever need anything from the pet store or even just need someone to talk to, stop by my shop. I'm happy to help in any way I can."

"Same here," Gray said, shaking the guy's hand. "When your mom's feeling a little better, bring her by my shop. I'll give her a complimentary haircut." Gray smiled again, genuinely this time. "Hopefully, this mess will be over soon and I'll be back open for business."

"Thanks, both of you," Tim said, waving from the front porch as they made their way back to Issy's beat-up old truck.

As they climbed inside Brown Betty, Gray ran through what they'd just learned from Tim in his head. He sat on the passenger seat and shut the door. "I doubt Tim's our killer. Unless he was lying, he had no motive to want to hurt Eric. The guy was investigating a case for him."

"He seemed honestly upset by the news of Eric's murder. Plus he's a good guy taking care of his mom like that. It's a big sacrifice." Issy closed her door and then clicked her seatbelt into place before starting the engine. "So what next? Should we talk to Beth Wilkins?"

Gray wasn't looking forward to that conversation. No one was sure what had caused Beth Wilkins's plunge off the deep end, but she was definitely nuts. Trying to get useful information out of her would be a challenge. He sighed and rubbed his eyes, the pressure of the day settling on his shoulders and seeping inside him as bone-deep exhaustion, and it wasn't even after five yet. "Guess we'll be stopping at O'Hara's Pub then. That's where she usually hangs out this time of day."

"No, I think we should wait until tomorrow." Issy gave him a quick glance, and Gray's tense shoulders relaxed a tad. "You look as if you've been hit by a freight train. I think it's best you go home and get some rest tonight. We can catch her earlier in the day tomorrow, when she's more on the sober side, and hopefully gather a few more clues before we talk to her. Sound good?"

"Sounds good." Gray watched the scenery pass as they headed back toward downtown. The first buds were starting to appear on the trees, and the daffodils were just starting to peek from the ground. "Instead of sitting at home alone, though, can we meet at your fire pit tonight? I'll bring the marshmallows and graham crackers for the first s'mores of the season, and we can hash out more about Eric's death."

"That's fine." She reached over and patted his arm. "It's all going to be okay, don't worry. I'll let Raine and Ember know and have Ember bring the chocolate." Issy signaled and then turned the corner near the town square. "Should I call DeeDee as well? What about Dex?"

"Yep. The whole gang." Gray opened the door once they pulled up to the curb in front of his salon. Looked like the police had cleared out for now, but there was still yellow crime scene tape up everywhere. Not exactly good for business or his reputation. "Invite them all. Maybe Dex and DeeDee can fill us in on what's happening with the police investigation."

CHAPTER 6

As promised, that night, all the Quinn cousins gathered around the fire pit in back of Issy's cottage on the lake, along with Issy's boyfriend Dex and all their familiars. Gray loved these nights together. The air smelled of campfire and pine from the surrounding trees, and a soft breeze blew, carrying with it the hooting of owls and the crisp scent of the lake. The last streaks of pink from the sunset hovered near the horizon, back-lighting the layers of blue mountains in the distance. It was springtime, and the nights were still cool in northern New Hampshire, so they all wore jackets and tucked plaid fleece blankets in their laps to ward off the chill.

Across the flickering fire, Issy and her boyfriend Dex fed each other gooey toasted marshmallows. Gray's heart swelled with happiness for his cousin. He pushed away a twinge of jealousy. So what if he didn't have anyone special? He could still be happy for Issy.

It was funny. At first, Gray hadn't been so sure about Dexter Nolan and whether he'd be good enough for Issy, but he'd turned out to be an okay guy, despite working for the FBPI — the Federal Bureau of Paranormal Investigations. Dex was an agent, which technically made the Quinns his enemies, yet he and Issy had fallen in love. He'd yet to turn any of them in, and he and Issy seemed really happy together.

Dex treated Issy well, which was most important to Gray. Plus, he supposed, it was good Issy had fallen for the guy, because it gave them a friend in the bureau. They needed one, considering Dex's boss, Stanley Judge, was a real pain in everyone's butt. A stickler for rules and gunning to find a paranormal, Stan had cut things a bit too close for Gray's comfort several times already. He only hoped he wouldn't have to endure questioning by that guy before this was all over.

"How's Stan?" Gray asked, doing his best to keep the snarky tone from his voice but failing miserably if everyone's collective snort was any indication. He chuckled and shoved his stick with the marshmallow impaled on the end into the flames. "Did he hear about the murder yet?"

"Oh, yeah. He did," Dex said, assembling his own s'more. "But I managed to convince him that it had nothing to do with paranormals. At least for now."

"That's good," Issy said from beside him, reaching over to steal a square of chocolate from his graham cracker. Dex smacked her hand away, then kissed her on the cheek. "The last thing we need is Stan coming here and poking around in Eric's case."

Now that Dex was assigned to Silver Hollow permanently, Stan mostly stayed at the FBPI offices in Ohio. That was just fine with Gray. The farther away he stayed, the better. Stan flew in only when he thought there might be a paranormal to capture. Hopefully Dex would keep him convinced that there was nothing going on in Silver Hollow that warranted his personal attention.

"Ursula might be disappointed, though." Ember laughed, tucking the edges of her blanket more firmly around the kittens in her lap. "She and Stan seemed to be getting pretty friendly on that last case. I thought she might keep him under her thrall for a while longer."

Ursula Lavoie, a vampire, was Silver Hollow's medical examiner. The last time Stan was in town, everyone noticed he'd been looking unusually pale and spending an unusual amount of time at the morgue. Gray smiled to himself. It would certainly be ironic if the great paranormal hunter ended up being turned into a paranormal himself.

Raine grinned, a rarity for her these days. "Yeah. Maybe it wouldn't be such a bad idea to have Stan stop by the morgue and fall victim to her spell. With Dex and

Stan on our side, we'd never have to worry about the FBPI again."

Gray pulled his marshmallow from the fire and blew out a stray flame before making his own s'more. "Can't say I'd be disappointed by that outcome."

"How'd your visit with Tim Stevens go?" Dex asked around a bite of graham cracker.

"Not very enlightening, I'm afraid. He hired Eric to look into some insurance investigating for his mother." Gray broke off a bite of s'more for Cosmo, who was waiting patiently on his shoulder. The bird nibbled the treat, sending a cascade of crumbs down the front of Gray's black windbreaker. "Hopefully we'll have more luck with Beth Wilkins, though she's not exactly stable. I wish we had some way to make her more lucid, at least for a little while."

"I can bring along a soothing plant when we visit tomorrow. That should get her to relax and tell us what we need to know." Raine pulled her phone from the front pocket of her overalls and began typing a note into it. "I've sent myself a reminder. I'm free tomorrow for lunch if you guys want to go then."

Gray, Issy, and Ember all checked their calendars.

"Works for me," Ember said.

"Me too," Issy agreed.

"Me three." Gray finished adding it to his calendar, doing his best not to be disappointed at just how free his schedule was at the moment. If he really stopped to think how much money he was losing each day the salon was closed, he'd fall into a pit of despair. Thankfully he was wise with his money and had sufficient funds saved to tide him over for a few months.

The sound of a car door slamming was followed by the crunch of boots on gravel. DeeDee walked around the corner of the cabin moments later. She was late, an unusual occurrence for her, and Gray couldn't resist teasing her a bit about it. "Look who finally showed up. Get too busy with your new fiancé?"

DeeDee gave him a flat stare, clearly not amused. The blush in her cheeks gave her away. He was truly happy for her and her new man. Gray and DeeDee had a special relationship. They'd been friends for ages, and he took a bit of credit for bringing her and Caine together. He had cast one of his beauty spells on her at her request. Not that she'd needed it. She was lovely before, but now that she'd found her soul mate, she positively glowed.

That pang of yearning stabbed his chest again. He wondered if such a thing would ever happen for him. The thought was quickly chased by the sobering realization that no, it would not. Especially if he got himself arrested by Owen and punished by the tribunal for the murder of Eric Naill. Even more incentive to keep his mind on the investigation.

"Caine's busy in editing and postproduction, but he sends his greetings," DeeDee said.

She took a seat on the log beside Gray and grabbed

the bag of marshmallows, shoving one into her mouth without bothering to toast it first. "And I'm sorry to tell you guys, but Owen doesn't have anything new yet either. Just the same leads you've got — Tim and Beth. Oh, and he's filing for a search warrant for Eric's office. I'm guessing he's thinking along the same lines as the rest of us — that this has something to do with one of Eric's cases."

"He still doesn't know about us paranormals, though, right?" Ember asked.

"Of course not." DeeDee swallowed another marsh-mallow. "He's fixated on the evidence of the murder weapon being those golden shears of Gray's and why he didn't report the break-in right away." Gray winced, and DeeDee patted his back. "I know this is hard on you, buddy, but you need to know what's going on. Owen thinks it's odd the killer had your shears."

"So do I," Gray said, throwing up his hands in exasperation. Cosmo squawked and flapped his wings in commiseration. "If he only knew how hard it was for me to get those in the first place and how valuable they are to me, he'd know I'd never use them to kill anyone. I keep them secured in my drawer every night. Or at least I did ..." His shoulders slumped. "Gah! This is all such a mess."

"Are you sure they're yours? Maybe someone else had a pair?" DeeDee suggested.

"No such luck. They're rare, and I'm missing mine."

"Could someone else have taken them during the day without you noticing?" Dex asked, playfully slapping Issy's hand away from his second s'more. "Shear Magic is a madhouse during business hours. I've been in there. All those women running around primping and preening. I don't know how you keep it all straight on your own."

"I manage just fine." Gray frowned. "And no, no one could've taken them. I use those shears on every cut. It's what helps me create the perfect look for each client. If they'd gone missing, I'd know. Just like I noticed this morning."

"Well then." DeeDee reached over to scratch Cosmo's head, smiling and cooing to the cockatoo, who obviously loved every second of the attention. "Owen's willing to pursue other avenues if we can present him with some viable ones. You and Owen are friends, so I doubt he wants you to be found guilty any more than the rest of us do. The crime scene crew should be done the day after tomorrow, so you can at least reopen the salon for business after that. And I'll keep you posted on any new developments as best I can, buddy. Promise."

"That's good," Ember said. "I can't tell you how many customers I've had in Divine Cravings talking about that new haircut you gave Mrs. Newcastle. Every lady in town wants an asymmetrical style now. Way to start a new trend, cuz."

Gray snorted and shook his head.

"Well, I'll do my best to steer Stan away from this case. But you know how he gets when he thinks he's onto the scent of something," Dex said. "We all know you didn't do it, but he might want to fly out and be there to question you anyway."

"If he does, I'll be right there with you, buddy," DeeDee said. "We'll get through this."

"I wonder if this all really has something to do with the South Side Coven, like Luigi mentioned," Issy said. "I mean, we know it's a paranormal killing, but why Eric Naill? And why would someone want to frame Gray for the murder?"

"I don't know." Gray sighed and checked his messages on his phone. Still no response from Switzerland. If he couldn't get another pair of magic shears, it wouldn't matter much if his shop was open again. Without them, he'd be just another okay stylist.

Self-doubt joined the tension already knotting inside him. An image of Starla, as she'd looked earlier in her store, flashed through his mind, and he made a mental note to talk to Brimstone about setting up a meeting with her. He wasn't sure why, but his gut told him he needed to see her to get answers.

That tingle of connection sparked inside him again before he shook it off. The last thing he needed right now was an ill-advised, unwanted attraction to the one woman he could never have a relationship with, at least not in the present climate between the North and South covens in Silver Hollow. "I don't know. I just want this all to be over and things to get back to normal. Hopefully we'll find out something useful when we talk with Beth Wilkins."

CHAPTER 7

The next morning, Gray was up early as usual but found himself with nowhere to go. The salon was still closed for the investigation, so he felt a bit adrift. He'd still not heard back from the wizard about replacement shears. Without those, it would be a struggle to maintain his level of perfection for clients. Sure, he could cast a beauty spell here and there, but for lasting results, he needed those golden scissors. Which made him wonder why the killer had used those shears. They'd been inside the salon, so had the killer been in there too? Had Eric? Or had someone taken them out earlier and used them to frame him? How would they have gotten to them without him noticing?

He was sure those shears had been in his drawer. And there'd been no sign of a break-in, which meant that whoever had gotten to them had used magic to do it.

They already knew paranormals were involved from the smell of wax on the back door of his shop, but magical teleportation took a special skill set. So the killer had to be somebody magical. And powerful. Too bad that eliminated their two suspects. Tim wasn't magical, and Beth was too confused.

Unless Eric had broken into the salon. He could have magically opened the lock and then the killer followed him in. They fought, the killer grabbed the scissors as a weapon, and the fight progressed into the alley where the killer stabbed Eric, shut the door, and fled. So it could have been someone magical or someone not magical. That didn't narrow things down any at all.

He got ready then shuffled around his renovated ski cabin, made coffee, got Cosmo up and fed, even admired the view from his back deck. The cabin was perched halfway up a steep mountain, isolated in the woods with no other houses in sight. He had a panoramic view of the mountain range and Lake Winnipesaukee below. In winter he could ski right from his backyard. In summer he enjoyed all kinds of wildlife — deer, fox, owls, turkeys, moose, and even the occasional black bear.

He'd chosen this place specifically because of that view and the abundance of wildlife, but he rarely got to enjoy it, so this was a special treat — even if the circumstances behind his free time weren't ideal. He spent time on the deck listening to the hollow thunk of woodpeckers and contemplating the other aspects of Eric Naill's murder.

They still didn't have a suspect with clear motive. Unless maybe Beth did it out of anger. Luigi said she'd fought with Eric. With Beth's confused state of mind, Gray didn't think she'd stew about it and kill him later. More likely she'd have stabbed him during the fight. Then again, she did like to hang out at O'Hara's Pub, and the back door of their kitchen at the bar wasn't far from the rear exit of Gray's salon, where Eric had been killed. Maybe they'd argued again in the bar or Beth had seen him there and that had triggered her? Given her erratic behavior, Gray wouldn't be surprised if she'd lost it and killed Eric in anger.

He was getting nowhere, and all this thinking about the case was giving him a headache.

Cutting hair was his life, who he was. When that was taken away, even for a short time, he felt utterly lost. He checked his text messages for the umpteenth time, but still no response from Switzerland. He'd gotten confirmation his messages had been delivered, so the wizard must be contemplating his case, deciding whether Gray deserved a second pair of golden shears. Gray considered sending another message, another plea, but decided against it. All he could do now was wait.

Thankfully, someone knocked on the door and saved him from a slow death by tedium. He answered, expecting maybe one of his cousins had come over early to discuss their meeting with Beth later and what questions they would ask, but instead he found Luigi Romano on the porch.

Surprised, the warning bells in his head immediately sounded, but he didn't have much choice except to invite the guy in and offer him some coffee. After all, Luigi was a wizard himself and close with the local Wizard Council. His help could be invaluable in discovering who might have killed Eric Naill — unless the council had sent him to take Gray away.

Of course, his mind had immediately jumped to the thought that Luigi might have been the killer, but that made even less sense than the rest of the current suspects. Luigi was working hard to establish himself in Silver Hollow. He was a peacemaker, a sort of magical law enforcement officer. Plus he had a thriving pizza business to run. Gray couldn't see the guy throwing all that away to kill a PI he barely knew. Plus, he had no motive ... then again, so far, neither did anyone else.

Luigi came in, his duster swirling around him as he took a seat in one of the large, rustic leather armchairs in Gray's living room. Between his usual jeans and black shirt underneath and the scraggly beard, the guy looked more like a biker band wanna-be than a serious threat. Rumor had it Luigi had fallen out of favor with the committee, that his magic had been diminished. Was that why Luigi never carried his wizard's staff? Gray wasn't sure most wizards had theirs at all times; there were some who preferred to keep a low profile and never carried one.

Staff or no staff, the fact that Luigi had come to his home made Gray nervous. Had he come as a friend, or was he trying to pry out some information that the Wizard Council could use as evidence against Gray? Maybe catching Eric's killer would put Luigi back in good standing, and Gray was an easy fall guy. Maybe Luigi had killed Eric with Gray's shears for that very purpose.

Nah. He was getting paranoid. Best to keep things in perspective. Luigi had never done anything to make Gray think that he was malicious. He went into the kitchen to get their coffee while Luigi scratched Cosmo's head. "Nice place you got here, Graeme."

"Thanks. And please, call me Gray." He'd bought the cabin a few years back with plans to turn it into a show-piece during his off hours. Unfortunately, his off hours were few and far between these days, so the place still had a sort of rough, bare-bones kind of feel. He'd managed to restore a few of the original features, like the giant river-rock fireplace in the living room and the huge windows that looked out over the mountain. The kitchen was still torn up, and some of the walls were down to the studs, but it was clean and safe, and that's all that mattered to Gray at the moment.

He finished fixing a mug of brew for Luigi then refilled his own before taking them both into the living room. He handed Luigi his mug and then took a seat on the leather sofa across from him. Cosmo flew over to perch on Gray's shoulder.

"So, what brings you by so early?' Gray asked, feeding Cosmo a slice of orange. "Any news about Eric Naill's murder?"

"Yeah, I got news," Luigi said, sipping his coffee. "Came by to let you know Martin Ellsworth is hot on this case. The death of a wizard is no small matter, and Martin wants it solved fast. The Wizard Council, of course, is backing him one hundred percent."

"Of course." The local Wizard Council considered themselves above the other witches and covens in the area, which didn't always sit well with other magical folk. "Has he found any new evidence?"

Luigi gave him a pained look. "No, but you're his prime suspect right now."

Gray put his mug down on the heavy oak coffee table between them, his hands shaking slightly. It wasn't unexpected, seeing as it was his shears that had been used as the murder weapon. Gray had hoped his reputation of being a good guy would have lent him some credibility. But no, apparently one could live a whole life not causing trouble and become a prime suspect just on one piece of evidence. Luigi watched him closely, his dark eyes not unkind.

"I'm sorry, man," Luigi said, sighing. "I imagine this is pretty rough on you."

"You've got no idea." Gray raked a hand through his hair and sat back. "I mean, I don't even have a motive."

Luigi shrugged. "Right now, all they have is the murder weapon. Hopefully, as the investigation continues, they'll find something that points in another direction and focus on other suspects."

He couldn't really blame Luigi. He appreciated the fact that he'd come over to give him the update. It seemed he really was here trying to help instead of making the Quinns look bad in front of the tribunal, so that was something. And rumor had it his input had helped get Karen Dixon out of trouble with the committee and gave her the chance to start her juice bar. Put that all together, and Luigi seemed far more an ally than an enemy.

"Is there anything at all that you found the day Eric died?" Luigi asked. "Anything you maybe didn't mention to the cops that might help point to who really did this?"

Gray thought for a moment. "Issy said she smelled wax on the back door of my salon. So whoever tried to break in used magic. They also may have used teleportation to get those shears out of my locked drawer. I'm not sure if anyone actually entered my shop, but nothing was out of order. I did sense something odd when I opened up that morning, but I could never nail down what it was. Maybe a death aura, or maybe something did happen in the shop. I can't be sure."

"Interesting," Luigi said, stroking that long beard of

his, his expression contemplative. Luigi frowned. "Why though? Why your shop? Why your shears? I mean, your salon is nice and all, but why would someone try to break in there to use your pair of magical scissors to kill Eric Naill? Then leave his body in the alley behind your shop? Obviously, if they were trying to frame you, it all makes sense. You got any enemies, Gray? Or maybe the Quinns have a feud going with another coven? Maybe someone on the South Side looking for a bit of retaliation?" Luigi seemed to think about that for a second and then shook his head. "Nah, it's all speculation right now. Best not mention any of it to Martin until we're sure. Sorry to say that most of it only makes you look worse, buddy."

"Worse?" Gray asked. "How?"

"Well, I got wind that Owen is looking at the self-defense angle, meaning you were working late in your shop and Eric tried to get in the back door for whatever reason. You caught him, a fight ensued, and you stabbed him. You could try to plead self-defense, but you're a big, healthy guy. Eric was smaller and shorter. Not exactly a fair fight."

"But that's not what happened. Not at all." Gray pushed to his feet, and Cosmo flew back to his cage in the corner. "I didn't kill anyone. I don't know why Eric was there or why anyone would want to kill him. I swear. Owen's going to bring me in for questioning, isn't he?"

"Probably before the end of the day. Just be prepared and be honest. I believe you, buddy. Owen wants to believe you too. We're on your side, remember? Calm down." Luigi finished his coffee and then stood. "Listen. I heard Ember and Raine talking about you guys going over to see Beth Wilkins this afternoon. I'd suggest you also do a little more investigating into Tim's father, Charlie Stevens. Like I said, he was involved in some kind of scandal shortly before he died. The facts surrounding what happened were never made public. I guess once he died, the Wizard Council didn't see any point to that. They didn't see any reason to make it harder on his family. I mean, they already had to close up his barbershop and all. Of course, his wife always insisted he didn't commit suicide, because she never knew about the scandal. In fact, she went a little crazy after his death, and it's only gotten worse over the years."

"Tim's father was a barber?" Gray felt a bond with the guy.

"Yep, one of Silver Hollow's finest back in the day, or so I hear." Luigi looked at him curiously. "You didn't know?"

"No, why would I?"

"Well, your salon is his old shop."

Huh. This case sure was full of surprises. And that explained why he'd gotten the place at such a good price and why it had been empty for decades. Gray had been a toddler when Charlie Stevens had died, so he guessed the scandal had been all but forgotten by the time he rented the place. No one would have mentioned it.

"I had no idea. I got a good deal on the place because the space had been empty for a while. I thought it was great at the time because of all the old-fashioned architectural details — the original black and white tile, the molded cornices and crown work, the whole retro vibe. There weren't any barber chairs or anything, so I guess I never thought about what was there before. I spent a lot of time cleaning it all up to restore the floor and walls to nearly brand-new condition." He shook his head. "I kept all of it, every detail, even though some of the floor tiles were chipped." He gave a sad snort. "There was one section where the workers had made a mistake. They put two black tiles together. It's not really noticeable now, though, since I covered it with a shelf of hair products and styling tools."

Luigi stroked his beard again, a sign he was thinking. "Wait a minute. I should have realized this before. If your salon used to be Charlie's barbershop and there was a scandal associated with him, I wonder if the two incidents are related."

"Could be," Gray said, his mind racing with the possibilities.

"Let me do a bit more looking into it, and I'll let you know." Luigi started for the door. "I should get going. Lots of prep work for the lunch crowd today. It's our weekly two-for-one special, and we're doing a special promo this week with Karen at the Main Squeeze. Get a slice, get a juice free. Thanks for the coffee, buddy." He turned, halfway out the door. "Hey, just so you know. I did try to point out other possible scenarios to Martin, but I'm not exactly in the best standing with the Wizard Council myself, so …" He shrugged. "Anyway, Martin's been a respected wizard in these parts for almost forty years, so his word is gold. Watch yourself around him, okay? And let me know how it goes with Owen later."

"Will do," Gray said, following him to the door.

Luigi smacked Gray on the shoulder before walking out onto the front porch. "Take care of yourself, buddy. If anyone asks, I was never here. Martin probably wouldn't like it. And get yourself a good alibi, buddy. You're gonna need it."

Gray waved then closed the door, leaning back against it with a sigh.

An alibi was going to be difficult, considering he'd spent the night Eric Naill died at his cabin alone. He went back to the kitchen and put the mugs in the dishwasher. First, he needed to be ready for the meeting with Beth Wilkins. Then he needed to prepare to be questioned by Owen and, hopefully, DeeDee. He only hoped Dex had convinced Stan Judge this case was none of his concern.

CHAPTER 8

That afternoon, they went to see Beth Wilkins, who, surprisingly, was not at O'Hara's Pub, but instead was at her seedy apartment on the outskirts of Silver Hollow. True to her word, Raine brought one of her magical plants along, guaranteed to be soothing and relaxing, at least that's what she claimed. Gray was dubious at best. Usually Raine's plants did produce magical effects, but he'd held the thing in his lap on the way over to see Beth while they'd ridden in Issy's truck, and it hadn't done a thing to ease his anxiety.

Still, the minute Beth clutched the potted pink petunia, she seemed calmer, if the way she lay down on her sofa was any indication. Gray frowned. He'd seen Raine use her plants on other people, and they never seemed to affect them quite so strongly. Then again, there was a good chance Beth was already under the influence of alcohol or drugs or both, not to mention her memory issues. She held the plant close to her chest, like a baby. It was more than a bit creepy.

Beth's dark hair, now streaked with gray, was pulled back into a messy bun, and her gray eyes were glassy. Gray thought that if you looked close enough, you could see that she'd once been beautiful, with her delicate bone structure and wide gaze. Now, though, there was a sadness to her, a wistfulness that made Gray yearn for his magical shears so he could ease her torment.

But the shears were gone, and there was no certainty he'd ever get another pair.

At least Beth seemed eager to talk. She started spilling her guts even before they asked any questions related to Eric Naill's murder.

"Oh my!" she said, staring up at Gray with wide eyes. "Is that an angel on your shoulder?"

He gave Cosmo a sideways look and shook his head. "Nope. Just my pet bird."

"Oh well. Doesn't matter." Beth toyed with the leaves of the small plant. "I was angry with him, you know. Eric Naill. So angry. Because of him, I didn't get my workman's comp claim approved." She scowled and pointed at her knee, which was swaddled in bandages and a thick brace. "Hurt it kneeling to repair the apple crusher at the applesauce factory last year, and it's never been the same since."

Gray glanced at his cousins then took a seat on a

threadbare chair across from her. Ember had brought along a batch of special chocolates containing a truth spell in case they needed them, but they sat untouched on the coffee table. "Eric did investigate a case for you then? For a workplace injury? Or did the insurance company hire him to follow you around, maybe make sure that you were really injured?" To Gray, it sounded like the latter, and if it had been because he'd proved she wasn't hurt enough to justify workman's comp, Beth might have been very angry indeed.

"Huh?" Beth scrunched her nose, her expression foggy again. "Eric who?"

Raine adjusted Beth's hold on the flowerpot, and Gray suppressed an eye roll — barely. Interrogating Beth wasn't easy. You never knew if she was going to be lucid. Still, the minute the pot rested against Beth's chest again, her eyes cleared.

"Oh no." Beth shook her head. "Eric wasn't working for the insurance company. And technically he never worked for me either. I wanted to hire him to fight my side of the case for me, but he refused. Said dealing with insurance companies was too much of a pain."

Gray sat forward. "Beth, we were told you argued with Eric. What happened after that?"

"Nothing." Beth stroked the leaves of the plant as if it was a furry animal. "I got mad at him and yelled a bit. Then I left." She sat up and frowned, her face clouding over again as she lowered the pot to her lap. "At least I think that's what happened. My memory's kind of fuzzy now. Sometimes I forget recent events and sometimes I forget things that happened in the past." Her smile turned fond and wistful. "In fact, two nights ago when I was at O'Hara's, I saw Martin at the barbershop again, just like old times. Such fun we had."

Her eyes drifted closed, but Gray wasn't done. "Speaking of the good old days, Beth, do you remember anything about Charlie Stevens doing anything underhanded?"

"Underhanded?" She looked confused. "I'm not sure ..."

Gray glanced up at his cousins. He'd told them about Luigi's visit and the scandal concerning Charlie Stevens. "Like something illegal or scandalous, maybe?"

Suddenly Beth looked at Gray with suspicion. Had she been involved in the scandal? Heck, maybe she'd been involved with Charlie Stevens — he'd been married at the time — and *that* was the scandal. But then what did that have to do with the South Side witches? And if she was involved, would she even remember? Could that be the cause of her memory loss? Had she done something that she wanted to forget?

"I don't know anything about anything illegal." Beth seemed agitated. She clearly wasn't going to tell Gray anything about a scandal even if she did know. Gray decided to change course.

"Beth, if you were at O'Hara's that night, did you see

Eric there too? He was found behind my shop, and that's near the pub. I could really use your help to find out what happened. Please."

"Nah," she said drowsily. "I didn't see Eric again after I left his office. Not after our argument." She opened her eyes, looking as lucid again as Gray had ever seen her. "But I'll tell you something. If you want to know who else had a beef with Eric, check with Bobby Knight. He and I used to be friends, you know. Really good friends. More than friends." Sadness turned down the corners of her mouth, and her gaze went distant. "At least I think we did. Hard to remember now. I know it's bad to hang with the South Side witches, but back then, there was a summer when there was a truce and it wasn't considered to be such a bad thing. Bobby used to be so sweet to me. Such a handsome guy, and so romantic. Anyway, I saw him coming out of Eric's office the day I went there to hire him, and Bobby looked real mad. Brushed right past me and didn't give me the time of day. Jerk!"

Beth closed her eyes again, and this time she fell asleep. Gray and his cousins left, closing the apartment door on her loud snores.

As they walked back to Issy's truck, Raine cooed softly to her little plant, telling it what a good job it had done. But Gray was barely paying attention. The story was starting to come together.

Luigi had mentioned something about the South Side witches. Bobby Knight had left Eric's office angry. There had been some kind of scandal. What that had to do with Eric being found dead outside Gray's shop he had no idea, but he did know one thing: He had to talk to Starla Knight and find out exactly what her uncle had been up to.

CHAPTER 9

"Well, that was interesting," Ember said, taking a seat at a table on the patio outside the Main Squeeze Juice Bar. They'd stopped for lunch to decompress after speaking with Beth and to enjoy the sunny day. The interview with Beth hadn't taken nearly as long as Gray had expected, nor had it been nearly as informative as he'd wished. He'd wanted to stay longer and wake Beth up, ask her more about Bobby Knight and her relationship with him.

He still couldn't get Starla out of his head. The fact that someone else had tried a relationship that crossed that unspoken boundary and it had been successful — at least for a while — gave him a spark of hope that he now tamped down. He had no business thinking about dating anyone until he cleared his name and got his business back on track. Then he'd need to think long and hard about whether risking it all for a chance with Starla was worth it.

The juice bar was packed. He remembered what Luigi had told him earlier about the daily special and supposed that had something to do with it. He was glad the pizza shop was doing well, along with the juice bar. And if he could just relax, he might be able to enjoy this break. The girls still each had about a half hour left on their lunch breaks. Considering his salon was still closed for inspection by the police, Gray had all the time in the world. The idea didn't sit as well with him. He did his best not to glance across the square to where the yellow crime scene tape across the entrance to Shear Magic fluttered in the breeze.

"Interesting is one way to put it," Gray said, focusing on the case to distract himself. "The more I hear about Eric Naill, the more I think Luigi was right in saying the South Side witches are involved somehow, and this has something to do with the scandal Luigi mentioned. Especially since Beth ran into Bobby Knight, who was leaving Eric's office angry. It has to be a witch or a wizard who killed Eric. That's the only way I can figure someone got into my shop for the shears."

Raine set her plant on the table before her. "If it was a witch or wizard, that leaves Tim Stevens out."

Ember nodded. "But remember, whatever Beth said is suspect. She has memory issues and is under the influence of goddess-knows-what."

"Plus she lied to us," Issy said.

"How do you know that?" Ember asked.

"She said that Eric told her he wouldn't take her case because he didn't investigate insurance cases, but Tim Stevens hired him to look into his mother's insurance."

Raine frowned. "That's right. Do you think she lied about her reason for being angry to cover up the real reason because the real reason gives her a stronger motive?"

"Maybe." Issy sipped her drink. "Eric refusing to take her case doesn't seem enough to kill for, but with Beth's unstable state of mind, it might be. But if the argument was about something else, something important enough to kill over, she might lie to throw us off."

"Maybe *she* wasn't the one who lied," Raine said. "Eric might have lied to her about not taking insurance cases because he didn't want to get involved in her case."

"Who could blame him?" Issy asked.

"No one," Raine agreed.

"Maybe that real reason has something to do with the South Side witches and what happened back in the day with Bobby Knight," Gray said.

"But what did happen back in the day?" Issy asked.

Gray shrugged. "I have no idea. Luigi said it all got dropped when Charlie Stevens died."

"So Charlie Stevens was involved?" Raine asked.

"How?" Issy asked.

"Good question." Gray sipped the orange Creamsicleflavored juice drink in front of him. "The way Beth was talking, she and Bobby Knight had something going on. Maybe there was some problem with Charlie and Bobby over Beth."

Ember took the cover off her juice and squinted into the empty cup as if simply looking in there and wishing would fill it up again. "You mean like a love triangle or something?"

"Maybe."

"Who would kill Eric over an old love triangle?" Issy asked.

"I know it seems dumb now, but remember, back then, people were more straightlaced." Gray pointed out.

"Seriously?" Raine scrunched up her face. "It was only about thirty years ago, not the Middle Ages. Though I suppose if it was frowned upon to get romantically involved with the South Side and there was a love triangle with a married man going on that could have caused a scandal."

"And Eric might have discovered that and threatened both Beth and Bobby to make it public now," Gray said.

"Still seems kind of drastic to me," Issy said. "There must be more to it."

"Maybe there is another element — like if Bobby Knight is already on the outs with the Wizard Council, another mark against him could get his powers stripped," Raine suggested.

"Is he on the outs?" Issy asked.

"I have no idea. Just speculating as to why Bobby or Beth would be threatened if Eric discovered this old dirt on them."

"Beth isn't in her right mind. She might feel threatened by things that the rest of us think are nothing." Ember screwed up her lips. "And if Beth lied about the insurance claim as the reason she argued with Eric, she might also have lied about seeing Bobby Knight."

"You mean to frame him? I don't know about that. She didn't seem with it enough to be able to come up with a clever lie or plan to frame Bobby," Gray said.

"Yeah, she can barely hold a conversation. Not too much planning going on in that brain. She kept mentioning the 'old days,' and she said she saw Martin at the barbershop. What was that about?" Raine asked.

"Barbershop? We don't have a barbershop," Issy said.

It was true, there was no barbershop in town *now*, but Gray's cousins didn't know there had been one years ago.

"Used to be one where my shop is now," Gray offered. "So it makes sense she saw Martin there. Luigi mentioned to me earlier that Martin Ellsworth is heading up the investigation into Eric's death for the local Wizard Council, and he has his eye on Beth because she's been acting so erratically. He could have been following her that night, and she confused the present with the past."

"Ugh. That's even worse." Raine sighed, her frown deepening as she stroked a petunia petal. "If he's poking around your salon, then he's looking for evidence against you, Gray."

"True." He swallowed around the lump of anxiety that had returned to clog his throat. "But there's nothing I can do about that at present. My best bet is to keep looking for the real murderer. I'm innocent. I know that, so that means having Martin Ellsworth and Owen and anyone else who thinks they can solve this case sniffing around my salon to get this solved, then more power to them."

"We need to figure out what this scandal is about and what it has to do with Bobby Knight. If Eric was digging into something that Bobby didn't want dug up, he could be a suspect," Issy said.

"And let's not rule out Beth," Raine added. "The scandal had something to do with Charlie Stevens, who owned the barbershop. Beth mentioned something about it in reference to 'old times.'"

"Yeah, we can't rule her out. The only one mentioned in reference to the scandal that we can rule out is Charlie Stevens," Ember said.

"Unless he came back from the grave to kill Eric," Raine added.

"So who was around back then who might remember what the scandal was about?" Issy asked the group as she sipped her Tahitian Sunrise, a blue concoction laden with assorted tropical fruit juices and garnished with a colorful paper umbrella.

"I'm putting a garden in for Mr. and Mrs. Bryant later

today. They're pretty old. I'll see if they remember," Raine said. Sonya and Ken Bryant were elderly witches who had lived in Silver Hollow for what seemed like a hundred years. Maybe it *had* been one-hundred years given their special abilities to make youth potions. Sonya had her hair done at Shear Magic, and Gray knew her memory was sharp, and she noticed everything that went on in town.

"If anyone would remember, it would be Sonya Bryant. Thanks." Gray reached over to steal a hunk of pineapple from the skewer that had topped off Raine's drink and then fed it to Cosmo, who preened and nuzzled Gray's neck as he perched on the back of Gray's chair.

Bella danced around Issy's feet, wanting to be picked up, and Raine continued to talk to the little petunia plant as though the rest of them weren't there. Gray had asked her earlier why she hadn't brought her plant familiar, a Venus flytrap named Mortimer, and she said he was at the greenhouse sunning himself and didn't wish to be disturbed.

"I'm betting Beth and Bobby did know each other, from what she said. Pretty well, too. And her running into him at Eric's office sounds like too much of a coincidence."

"Agreed." Gray sat back and sighed. What he really needed was for Brimstone to get on the ball and arrange the meeting with Starla so he could find out what she knew about her Uncle Bobby's recent activities.

Bobby Knight ticked a lot of boxes on his list of primary suspects. The fact that Bobby was angry after his meeting with Eric suggested motive, and he was a well-known powerful wizard. Rumor had him doing everything from minor parlor tricks to incredible feats of transfiguration. Hype aside, Gray would bet Bobby would have no problem killing Eric. Now all he had to do was find out what their connection was.

Luigi delivered the pizza they'd ordered to their table. The smells of baked cheese, tomato sauce, and fresh, homemade crust made Gray's stomach rumble. He'd barely taken a bite of his first slice when Luigi pulled a chair up beside him.

"Hey, Gray. I wanted to warn you again that Martin's getting antsy." He glanced around to make sure they had privacy. The rest of the patio crowd had cleared out. "The tribunal is putting pressure on him to find the killer. Owen seems to think you're suspicious, so Martin thinks it would tie things up nicely if the police went ahead and arrested you."

"No!" Ember cried, her eyes wide. "They can't!"

"Unfortunately, they can. Or at least bring him in for questioning." Luigi sighed and sat back. "The good thing about Owen arresting Gray is that it would fall under the human jurisdiction, so if he's found guilty, he'll serve his sentence in human jail. That would also take care of things on the paranormal side, because it would allow the tribunal to put the matter to rest."

"*If* he's found guilty, which he won't be because he didn't do it. That's ridiculous." Issy swallowed a bite of pizza then wiped her mouth with a paper napkin. "Besides, no paranormal belongs in a human jail cell. I won't allow it. It's cruel and inhumane. We need to find out what's going on with Bobby Knight and his connection to this mess and get Gray's name cleared as soon as possible."

"How, though?" Raine asked around a bite of cheese. "It's not as if we can just take a stroll over to the South Side. Besides, we don't have any connections there."

"I do," Issy said softly, and Gray's heart skipped. "Well, sort of. Starla Knight, Bobby's niece. Gray and I talked to her at her jewelry shop during a previous investigation. Maybe we should take another trip back there and ask her."

"Oh, I don't think that's a good idea." Gray pushed his empty plate away, his stomach too knotted to even think about eating. "None of you should even think about talking to anyone on the South Side. This is my problem, and I won't have any of you punished for it. Understand?" He met the gaze of each cousin, and they nodded. "Good. I have a plan. And maybe we can manipulate Owen into helping us if I can find some evidence against Bobby Knight and have DeeDee or Dex feed it to Owen, and ..." Gray's speech was severed by the single bleep of a siren behind him. He turned to see Owen's squad car pulling up to the curb.

"Hey, Gray," Owen waved. "Got a few minutes to ride with me to the station to answer a few questions?"

Oh crap!

Gray tamped down the panic that rose in his chest. He didn't want his cousins to think he was frightened, or they might do something drastic. *Just act natural.* He nodded and pushed up from his chair. Best to get this over with and minimize the damage. People were already starting to stare and whisper and point at him on the patio. As he got into the back of the car, he glanced to the rest of the group at the table and gave them a reassuring nod, but judging by the terrified looks on their faces, it didn't do much to convince them that everything would be okay.

GRAY BUCKLED HIS SEAT BELT, and they took off for the station, Cosmo's wings flapping nervously as he perched on the back of the seat.

"I didn't do this," Gray said, staring at his hands in his lap. "I swear."

"I want to believe you," Owen said, looking particularly colorful today in a rainbow-hued Hawaiian shirt festooned with seagulls and beach balls, its jolly scenes at direct odds with Gray's current sorry state of affairs. "I do. But I'd be remiss if I didn't at least bring you in. You understand, right?"

"Right."

They arrived at the station a few minutes later and walked inside, past Myra Bell, the receptionist — who gave Gray a somewhat snooty, cold look totally uncalled for considering he'd done her last haircut for free — and headed straight back to an interrogation room, where DeeDee, Dex, and Stan Judge were waiting. DeeDee and Dex smiled when Gray walked in. Stan scowled.

So Stan had come out to Silver Hollow after all. This did not bode well for Gray. Now not only would he have to juggle the paranormal investigation with Martin and the normal investigation with Owen, he'd have to make sure Stan didn't want to haul him out to Area 59. Gray wasn't exactly sure what the FBPI did out there — some sort of paranormal testing — but he'd never heard of anyone taken there ever returning.

"Have a seat, buddy," DeeDee said, indicating the chair next to her. "We just want to clarify a couple of things with you."

"Yes," Stan said, his thin, pale face and ill-fitting suit making Gray think more of a mortician than a top agent for the FBPI. "I'd be most interested in hearing about how a pair of 24-karat gold scissors worth more than some people's homes ended up in the possession of a small-business owner who then used them to kill a private investigator."

Dex sat forward, the implied eye roll in his frown

nearly palpable. "All I want to know is how your scissors ended up in Eric Naill's back."

"I don't know. I wish I did, because it would make this so much easier." Gray sighed. "Honestly. I saw no evidence anyone broke in, so I have no idea how anyone got my scissors."

"I do." Stan gave him a look that would have made a church matron proud. "You took them yourself, stabbed Eric Naill, then went on your merry way."

"Why would I do that?" Gray snapped back, his patience at an end. "Do give me some credit. If I was going to kill someone, first I'd need to have motive, which I don't. I barely knew Eric Naill. I had no reason to kill him. Second, why would I use my own precious shears to do him in, then leave them there — along with the body — for anyone to find? Doesn't make any sense at all."

"He could've startled you when he tried to break in," Stan sputtered. "Crimes of passion rarely involve logic."

"Crimes of passion? As I said, I barely knew the guy, and contrary to popular myth, some of us hair stylists are straight. I prefer women. And there was no sign of a break-in, right?" His angry gaze flicked to DeeDee, who nodded. She bit her lip, her eyes sparkling with amusement as she clearly tried to bite back a laugh. "Next question."

"Who do you think killed the guy?" Owen asked from where he stood, leaning against the wall, arms crossed.

"Anybody with a grudge against you who'd like to see you framed for murder?"

"No one I know of." Gray exhaled slowly. He couldn't come out and say what his real suspicions were with Stan the Man sitting there and Owen having no idea about the paranormals in the area. So he tried a different route. "I spoke to Beth Wilkins earlier today. She said she saw a man named Bobby Knight coming out of Eric Naill's office the day she went there to hire him for a case. She said Mr. Knight seemed angry."

Owen gave a curt nod toward DeeDee, who scribbled down the name, her expression blank. "Okay. I'll look into him. And where were you the night Eric Naill was killed, Gray?"

"At home. Alone." He managed to hide his wince, barely.

"Can anyone corroborate that?" Owen asked. "Any witnesses who might have seen you there?"

"Other than my cockatoo Cosmo?" Gray asked, his shoulders slumping. "No."

Everyone looked at the bird now perched on the back of Gray's chair. Cosmo bobbed his head up and down as if agreeing with Gray's statement that he was home all night, but that didn't seem to convince Stan or Owen.

"How would this Bobby Knight even get your scissors?" Stan asked.

"I have no idea." Gray couldn't very well tell him about teleportation. Should he suggest someone could have swiped them during the day unnoticed? Was teleportation the paranormal version of that? But he'd already said that it would be almost impossible for anyone to take his shears. He glanced at DeeDee for help.

"It's impossible to know how someone got the scissors, but I was hoping we could rule out Gray — and other suspects — another way. Ursula is conducting re-enactments of the murder. You know, trying to figure out how tall the killer might have been based on the angle and penetration of the blade. That might help," DeeDee offered.

Stan perked up at the mention of the medical examiner. "Ursula Lavoie? Maybe I should go over there and witness these re-enactments."

"I think that's a good idea, Stan." Dex gave DeeDee a raised-brow glance as Stan stood up, nearly dropping his notepad in his haste.

"Yeah, I'll report back." Stan breezed out, and they all watched him leave in silence.

"Okay, then." Owen pushed away from the wall. "I think that's enough questions for now. Thanks for your time, Gray. We'll be in touch. Oh, and best you stick around the area until this is all cleared up, eh?"

CHAPTER 10

*D*ex dropped him off back in town and, after answering the frantic texts from his cousins wondering if he'd been arrested, Gray walked around the town square, stopping in front of Shear Magic. The shop looked deserted. The crime scene tape still hanging over the entrance gave it a foreboding air. The lights inside were off, and the "closed" sign was on the door, just as he'd left it.

He couldn't shake the feeling of violation, knowing the police had been in there rooting around in his belongings. He hoped they hadn't made too much of a mess. He stepped closer and cupped his hands to peer through the front window. Cosmo squawked and pecked at his reflection in the glass.

From what Gray could see through the shadows

inside, things had been moved around quite a lot. Shelf units had been pushed into different spots, product had spilled off the shelves or tipped over, and even his work station had been thoroughly set askew. He'd have major cleanup to do before he could open again. *If* he could open again. He pulled out his phone again to check for a message from Switzerland, but there was nothing.

Feeling more than a little dejected, he walked along the alley to check out the back entrance area and discovered Martin Ellsworth poking around the rear door. Perfect. Just the person he needed to see to top off his dismal afternoon. As if getting grilled by the police and Stan Judge wasn't enough. Crime scene tape still covered this area too, and the chalk outline on the ground was still bright and visible, a not-so-pleasant commemoration of the events that had taken place here.

Martin turned at the sound of Gray's footsteps. His long, gray-streaked brown hair was tied back with a black ribbon into its usual ponytail. Gray hesitated. Martin had a reputation as a powerful wizard, and the long ponytail proved it. Wizards were fond of their hair, measuring their importance by its length. Gray was a witch, not a wizard, but he kept his own black hair at shoulder length not to prove his powers but just because he liked it that way.

Male witches could choose, if they wished, to pursue advanced studies in magic to become wizards. Gray had never felt inclined to do so, happy with his skill set and putting his magic to good use in the salon. Because of his choices, he'd been looked down upon on occasion by the local Wizard Council, which felt that any male witch worth his salt should want to be a wizard. Gray didn't care. He had enough friends and family surrounding him for support. Though today, it probably wouldn't have hurt to have closer ties to the council.

"What are you doing here?" Martin asked, his tone brisk and cold. He tapped his crooked burlwood wizard's staff against the ground as if emphasizing each word. His brown duster, newer and less worn than Luigi's, ruffled around him in the breeze. With his skinny form and craggy features, the guy reminded Gray of a gnarled magician from some fantasy movie, though he couldn't have been more than a decade or so older than Gray. Maybe having all that power inside a man aged him faster. If so, he was glad he'd never joined the Wizard Council.

"Returning to the scene of your crime?" Martin gave him a condescending, snooty look, obviously one of the faction who felt they were better than Gray because he was a mere witch.

"No." Gray straightened to his full height, which was several inches taller than Martin, and bit back a smile as the older man took in the size and breadth of him. Steady workouts and healthy eating had their advantages. "I came by to check if the police were done with their investigation. As a business owner, I have every right to be here. And as I told Owen earlier, if I was going to kill Eric, I would hardly do it behind my place of business, then leave both my shears and the body for anyone to find. I'm not a wizard, but I'm smarter than that."

Martin harrumphed and turned back to the door. "We'll see."

Gray ignored the snarky remarks and stepped gingerly around the dark splotches on the pavement and the chalk outline to reach the rear door. He swallowed against the constriction in his throat and decided to take his chances, asking a few more questions of Martin while he had the opportunity. Cosmo's claws dug into his shoulder, his yellow comb standing straight up atop his head, responding to the tension coiling inside Gray. "I heard Eric might have been here investigating a case that got him into trouble. Perhaps someone thought he was getting too close to a discovery. They could have followed him here and killed him."

"Why would they leave him behind a hair salon?" Martin asked, not looking at him, his pointed nose practically stuck inside the lock on the door. "Makes no sense."

"What else would they do with him?" Gray shrugged, going for casual but ending up feeling awkward and stiff. "Eric's investigation could have led him to another shop in this area. Several of the other businesses have exits leading out into this alleyway. Eric could have been stabbed elsewhere and then stumbled here and fallen before he died. There's another theory for you to check out. And speaking of theories, have you spoken to Beth Wilkins about all this?"

Martin straightened and fixed Gray with an icy glare, his dark eyes glittering like obsidian beneath the afternoon sun. "No, I haven't. And I don't need or want your theories anyway, Gray Quinn. I can smell that this door was opened by magic, plain as day. And for your information, I was in O'Hara's Pub the night Eric was killed, trailing Beth Wilkins to make sure she didn't do anything crazy — or anything *else* crazy. With her erratic behavior lately, she ended up getting into a fight with Eric, but afterward, I saw Eric walking down the street alone. No one followed him. That puts a tidy end to your hunch of him being stabbed elsewhere and dying here. Besides, logic dictates the person with best access is the shop owner with a door that leads right out to the exact spot where Eric's body was found."

"Wait a minute," Gray protested. "You said you were trailing Beth that night, at O'Hara's?" Luigi had mentioned that Martin was looking into Beth because she'd been acting erratically, but what if there was another reason? What if Martin suspected her erratic behavior had something to do with Eric's death?

"What of it?" Martin scowled.

"Is that because I'm not the only suspect you're investigating?"

"Maybe not the *only* suspect," Martin said, sniffing derisively, "but you're certainly the *prime* suspect. I'd start setting your affairs in order, Gray Quinn, because if I get my way, you're going to jail for a long time for the murder of Eric Naill."

CHAPTER 11

Gray's phone buzzed with a text from Raine a few hours later. He'd been moping around Silver Hollow, not wanting to go home but not really having a clear destination in mind. He'd been hoping to run into Brimstone and ask if he could arrange a meeting with Starla Knight. The cat had a knack for showing up when he didn't want him but was never around when he did.

He'd left the alley shortly after his confrontation with Martin Ellsworth, haunted by the misguided determination in the other man's eyes. Martin felt Gray was guilty, and nothing was going to sway his opinion on that matter. Sick dread coiled tighter in his gut. Setting his affairs in order was the least of his worries right now.

First he needed to clear his name. Then he needed to get a new pair of magical shears to replace the ruined ones, or there wouldn't be much in the way of affairs to set in order. Sure, he could continue to run a regular, nonmagical salon, but his profits would soon dwindle when the clientele realized his gifts were gone.

He'd travel to Switzerland and crawl on his hands and knees if it meant getting a new pair.

Squinting against the afternoon sun, he stared down at his phone screen to read Raine's message. She'd finished at the Bryants' and had some interesting news. She was backlogged with paperwork and new deliveries that afternoon and couldn't leave her shop, so she asked if Gray could come to her instead. He headed right over to see her.

The shop was as eclectic as Raine herself, with cute green-and-white-striped awnings outside and thriving plants everywhere. With all the misters and humidity from the attached greenhouse in back, it felt more like a rainforest inside than the middle of Silver Hollow, New Hampshire. He'd barely made it into the store, Cosmo bobbing and weaving on his shoulder, when Raine came from the back of the shop, her dark-green overalls splotched with dirt and her straight copper hair coming loose from her braids from working in the greenhouse.

She waved Gray into her tiny, cluttered office and closed the door behind them. The window was cracked to let in a bit of fresh air, and Raine's familiar, Mortimer, sat on the sill, soaking up the sun. She took a seat behind her desk, and Gray cleared off a chair in front of it.

Raine studied him from the other side of her desk, a mischievous glint in her eye that he hadn't seen since that misadventure they'd had with the demon. It was a good sign that Raine was getting back to her old self, but he'd enjoy knowing that much more if he knew he wasn't going to be forced to watch her recovery from a jail cell.

"What's going on?" Gray leaned over to allow Cosmo down off his shoulder to walk among the stacks of papers scattered atop the desk. "You found out something good, didn't you?"

Raine tried to plaster an innocent look on her face, but Gray could tell she was bursting to tell him something.

Raine played with the pencil on her desk, turning it over from end to end. "Sonya Bryant was a wealth of information. She and Ken used to keep abreast of all the happenings in Silver Hollow. Not so much now that they are older, but back in Charlie Stevens's day, they were in their prime." She glanced up from beneath long lashes at Gray. "In fact, she's second cousin to Martin Ellsworth, so she was privy to things most others didn't know about."

The mention of Martin Ellsworth was a reminder of just how determined Martin was to pin the murder on Gray and how little time he had to clear himself. He tamped down his impatience. It was best to let his cousin tell him in her own way. Despite the fact that he was desperate to know if she'd discovered anything that could clear his name, he liked seeing the enthusiasm that had been missing all these months. "So they know something that could help us?"

Raine nodded. "Sonya remembered there was a scandal involving Bobby Knight back in the day with guess who …?" Raine sat back in her chair looking like a cat that had just pilfered a bowl of cream.

"Beth Wilkins?" Gray guessed.

Raine nodded and leaned forward. "And guess what else."

Gray raised a brow, but this time she rushed on without making him guess.

"Charlie Stevens was messed up in it too."

Squawk! The plot thickens, boss, Cosmo telepathed, the yellow crest on his head sticking straight up as he looked at Gray with dark, concerned eyes.

Gray leaned back in his chair. "So Bobby Knight, Beth Wilkins, and Charlie Stevens had some kind of a love triangle?" Gray remembered Beth saying something about her and Bobby being real close, but she never said anything about Charlie Stevens. But Charlie had been dead for so many years now that maybe she'd forgotten about him.

"There were rumors about Beth and Bobby and a third person. Probably Charlie." Raine leaned practically halfway across her desk, the mischievous glint in her eyes brightening. "But there was something else. Sonya was at a party with Martin back then, and she overheard him talking about something he was investigating. Something worse than a love triangle."

Now they were getting somewhere. Gray hardly thought a decades-old love triangle was worth killing over. Unless Bobby had killed Charlie so he could have that all to himself. But if that were the case, how did Eric get involved? Had he stumbled across something that proved Bobby was a killer?

"Something worse?" Gray prompted.

Rain nodded. "Black-market toad warts."

"What?" That set Gray back a bit. Toad warts were a crucial ingredient for many powerful spells, but collecting them had been outlawed at the turn of the century. The method of obtaining them was incredibly cruel to the toads. Punishment for being found guilty of dealing in them was heavy.

Maybe he'd been chasing the wrong hunch the whole time and this had nothing to do with Beth and Bobby and everything to do with the black market. Bobby had always liked to push the envelope. Had Eric somehow discovered that Bobby had been involved in dealing illegal toad warts and threatened to turn him in?

Raine nodded. "Yeah. Now that's worth killing over."

"Wow! Okay." He frowned. "Huh. Perhaps that's why Charlie Stevens killed himself. Maybe he got caught and didn't want to bring that kind of shame on his family, not to mention the painful punishment to himself."

"Maybe. But if that's the case, why did someone kill

Eric?" Raine narrowed her gaze, tapping her fingers on the desktop. "Unless Eric's death has nothing to do with this."

"Seems like too much of a coincidence with all the suspects," Gray said. "So maybe Charlie Stevens didn't kill himself. Maybe he was involved with the toad wart scandal and wanted out, or he discovered someone else was involved and threatened to tell."

"And they killed him and made it look like a suicide," Raine concluded.

"Yep. And that leaves two people we know of who were involved," Gray said, "Bobby Knight and Beth Wilkins."

"That could be the reason behind Beth's memory loss — guilt," Raine said.

"It's too bad we can't get a straight story from her. We can't even question her and try to trip her up."

Raine sighed. "That leaves Bobby Knight, and since he's a Southie, we can't talk to him either."

"True." Gray pushed up from his seat. Now that he had something solid to dig into, he felt he finally had a good chance of finding out who really killed Eric and why. "Good thing I know of a way to get in contact with someone who is almost as good as talking to Bobby Knight himself."

CHAPTER 12

$\mathcal{W}$hen he returned to his cabin, Gray found Brimstone waiting for him on the porch. His mind still swirled with the new information Raine had given him, and he narrowly avoided stepping on the cat, who sat square in front of the door, grooming himself as if that was a perfectly legitimate place to attend to one's personal habits.

"I've been looking for you," Gray said.

"You and about a dozen female kitties," Brimstone muttered, too busy grooming himself to look up.

After a few moments of waiting for the feline to move out of the way, Gray issued a long-suffering sigh. "Any time you're finished, I'd love to talk about something important with you."

Brimstone gave him a pointed stare, his hellfire-orange eyes brimming with attitude. "The things we guys have to do in the name of justice."

"Excuse me?" Gray fiddled with his keys, scowling. "What are you talking about?"

"This meeting you wanted with Starla Knight." Brimstone flicked a piece of orange fur from his cheek with his paw. "It's on for tonight."

Gray raised a brow. Had the self-absorbed cat known what was on his mind? "I'm sorry?"

"A meeting. You. Starla Knight. This evening." Brimstone stood and gave a long, leisurely stretch. "Do try to keep up. I've been keeping an eye on this Eric Naill murder case, and you're going to want to talk to her about Bobby Knight. He's involved in this somehow, though perhaps not in the way you imagine. And setting up this rendezvous wasn't easy, believe me." Brimstone looked down his snout at Gray. "I hope you appreciate my efforts on your behalf. Trying to convince that orange tabby of hers to agree to coaxing her mistress to come tonight took all my powers of persuasion, but she finally gave in. You are to meet Starla in the neutral woods at dusk."

Gray stared at the cat for a moment, his pulse quickening at the thought of seeing the woman who'd been foremost in his thoughts again. But he wasn't prepared. He hadn't even considered what questions to ask. This probably wasn't a good idea at all. He should postpone it until later. "Any way we can reschedule? This evening isn't the best for me."

"Have you been sniffing too much hairspray again?" Brimstone quipped. "No, you can't reschedule. And yes, you need to be there. Trust me, with all fingers pointing at you for Eric's death, you want to be there. Tonight. In about twenty minutes, I'd say, based on the angle of the sun. Better hurry."

Brimstone raced off, leaving Gray alone with his panic.

With a sigh, he went inside and freshened up, fed Cosmo, and left him on his perch to rest before heading out to meet Starla. He'd changed into a clean pair of jeans and a black T-shirt, combed his hair, and brushed his teeth. His blood sizzled with an odd mix of adrenaline, anticipation, and apprehension. This could be his chance to find out if Bobby could have killed Eric Naill and clear his own name. It could also be a trap. On the plus side, he was going to see Starla again. On the down-side, he was going to see Starla again.

Tension coiled tighter than a cobra inside him.

The trees cast long shadows in the setting sun, and the woods took on an ominous, magical aura. Golden light filtered in, birds made their last flights home for the night, and squirrels scurried through the underbrush, grabbing the remaining acorns of the day. It was all so lush and serene it nearly made him forget why he was here.

He'd come alone, leaving Cosmo at home napping, one leg tucked up into his feathers, the other clutching his perch. At least he thought he'd come alone until he spotted a flash of charcoal fur out of the corner of his eye and saw Brimstone trailing him through the woods. Perhaps the snarky feline felt he had to watch over him because he'd set this whole thing up. Concern for others wasn't usually a high priority for Brimstone, with his sense of self-preservation always coming first, but the fact the cat seemed to think there could be danger ahead set Gray's own instincts on high alert.

As he neared the spot where he was to meet Starla, he scanned the area for signs of an ambush. Nothing seemed out of the ordinary. Then he spotted her, alone in a small clearing near the center of the woods, and his pulse raced for entirely different reasons.

She looked much the same as the last time he'd seen her — golden curls tumbling over her shoulders and down her back, lush curves hidden beneath her purple dress, a sweet smile on her pretty face as she stopped to speak with a chipmunk balanced on a log. His stiff shoulders relaxed a tad. She'd helped him once before, and maybe she'd do so again. And maybe the South Side Coven wasn't the enemy he'd always been led to believe. At least right now, looking at Starla, it didn't seem that way.

He stepped into the clearing, and she glanced over at him, looking as startled as he felt. Up close, she was even lovelier than he remembered. Creamy, smooth skin, bright midnight-blue eyes, and full pink lips. His breath caught as she stepped closer. He was enchanted.

"Elvira said you needed to talk to me," Starla said, her voice quiet. The setting sun cast long streaks of deepening purple and indigo across the rapidly darkening sky. The first stars twinkled overhead, and the crescent moon was just starting to rise over the crest of the White Mountains in the distance. The whole space seemed magical and more than a tad romantic.

"Elvira?" Gray unstuck his tongue from the roof of his mouth long enough to ask. He had no idea who Elvira was or how she knew Gray wanted to talk to Starla.

"My cat."

"Oh." Gray stood awkwardly, not knowing what to say next.

"So ... long time no see, huh?" Starla gave a tiny chuckle, and he felt that husky sound all the way to his toes.

"Uh, yeah." Gray fumbled over his words, still taken aback by her beauty. For a man who made his living charming others, it was unsettling. Starla had him under her spell without even trying. He cleared his throat and looked away, steeling himself against her powers. "Not sure if you've heard about all the stuff going on because of Eric Naill's murder."

Her pretty smile faltered, and she sat on a log. "I have. That's why I came. I want to help my Uncle Bobby.

I heard he was a suspect, and I don't want him to get in trouble. He's a good man and would never have killed Eric."

The words "good man" weren't ones he usually associated with Bobby Knight, but he supposed it depended on one's perspective. To Gray, the guy was a prankster, a bully, a wizard who'd reputedly used his powers against the North Side Coven at every opportunity. To Starla, Bobby was a beloved uncle, taking care of his own and protecting the South Side Coven in whatever ways he could.

And that line of thinking was getting him nowhere. He needed to concentrate on why he was here — getting answers to his questions about Eric's murder — and forget the rest.

Gray stood a few feet away, leaning against the trunk of an ancient oak, watching Starla. She seemed sincere, but he'd learned a long time ago in his business that looks could be deceiving. Still, he took a chance and played a hunch, mentioning what he and Raine had discussed earlier. "What about the incident all those years ago with your uncle, Beth Wilkins, and Charlie Stevens? Some kind of a scandal?"

"Oh, that." A hint of pink colored Starla's cheeks in the moonlight, and Gray felt the crazy urge to stroke his fingertips across her skin to see if it felt as soft as it looked. "I don't know anything specific, really. Just that Bobby had a true love once, but something went wrong. I heard their relationship had been forbidden, and Bobby never found anyone else."

Gray's chest squeezed at those words, the irony of the situation not lost on him. Starla had stirred similar interest in him that day in her shop. He'd been mesmerized, transfixed, awash in the knowledge that his connection with this woman transcended mere attraction and awareness to something more, something deeper, even though they barely knew each other. But he'd backed off because of the differences between them. Still, he couldn't stop thinking about her. The thought that he and Bobby might have more in common than he'd originally imagined left him a bit unsettled.

"He's been lonely for years," Starla continued, her tone quiet. "And now Bobby's grown angry and bitter. He blames the feud for what happened."

A pang of regret stabbed deep into Gray's gut. The last thing he wanted was to end up the same way Bobby Knight had, but there was no way a relationship between him and Starla could work. There were too many things stacked against them, weren't there?

But Starla was talking as if the only thing bothering her uncle was an old love that he couldn't have. Did she know nothing about the toad warts, or was she playing him for a fool? "Is your uncle bitter enough to stab a guy looking into his past?"

Starla frowned at him. "No. Absolutely not. My uncle refuses to talk about what happened back then. But what does it have to do with what happened to Eric? My uncle might have made some mistakes, but he's no killer."

"Why did he go to see Eric then?" He met her surprised stare. "Beth Wilkins claims to have seen him at Eric's office the day she went to discuss another matter with Eric. She says when Bobby left he was angry, as though he and Eric had argued. Do you have any idea what they were meeting about?"

"No. I didn't even know he went there, let alone that he and Eric argued." Starla wrapped her arms around herself as a chilly breeze swept the clearing, her filmy lavender chiffon dress little protection against the cold. Gray cursed himself for not thinking ahead and wearing a jacket he could lend her for warmth. "Not sure I'd trust what Beth Wilkins says, though. She's not right in the head these days. Stuck in the past. Not sure she even knows what she's talking about half the time."

"Maybe, but my sources tell me this all might be about something that happened long ago, and it has nothing to do with lost loves. It involves illegal magic."

Starla's eyes widened. She looked truly surprised, and in that instant, Gray knew deep down that she wasn't playing him. She had no idea what her uncle had been up to all those years ago. "Are you saying my uncle was into something illegal and that's why Eric was killed?"

Gray shrugged. He wasn't sure that Bobby Knight had been the one selling the toad warts. Maybe it had been Charlie or Beth. He didn't have the heart to tarnish Starla's image of the uncle she obviously cared about. "Maybe."

"Are you sure? I mean, I know he can be a prankster, but he's never done anything illegal. And as far as I know, he didn't have any problems with Eric Naill."

Gray sighed, moving to sit on the opposite end of the log to block some of the wind with his body. So far, this conversation had gotten him nowhere. "I'm not sure exactly what's going on, but I know Martin Ellsworth is trying to put the blame on me, and I certainly didn't kill Eric. Now, I'm not saying that your uncle is the one who did it, but his name has been brought up a few times. If he's as innocent as I am, then I need to get to the bottom of this and figure out who the real killer is, because if I don't we both may end up in jail." Gray turned to her. "I can't talk to your uncle, but anything you can do would help us both."

Starla gave him a small smile. Her scent — patchouli and jasmine — drifted on the night air to him. "I don't want anyone who is innocent to be prosecuted. Not my uncle. And not you. I'll try to find out why Bobby might have gone to see Eric and what they fought about if that will help."

"It will." Gray smiled back at her, clenching his fists to keep from reaching over to brush a stray curl from her cheek. Must be the hair stylist in him, though the way his fingertips tingled with the need to touch her, he knew that wasn't the case at all. He lowered his head and stared at the tips of his black boots. "And I'll do my best to find out more about this whole thing and let you know what I find." He held out his hand, thumb up, for a witches' handshake. "Deal?"

"Deal," Starla said, twining her thumb around his. Awareness sparked through Gray's system from their point of contact. "Should we meet back here again to discuss what we find?"

"Yep. Tomorrow night good for you?" He stood and brushed off his jeans. "Same time, same place?"

"Perfect." Starla stood and smoothed her hands down the front of her lavender dress, her pale skin glowing in the moonlight. She looked like some kind of fairy nymph come to life. "See you then."

"See you." They both stood for a moment, staring at each other, as if neither wanted to leave. Then, finally, Starla ducked away through the trees, disappearing into the darkness.

Gray watched for a long moment afterward, reluctant to head home but knowing he must. As he trudged back toward his cabin in the hills, he did his best to remind himself there could never be anything between him and Starla Knight, though for some reason it was getting more difficult to remember why.

GRAY TOOK the long way back to his car. He wanted to

be alone with his thoughts, and the cool night air was refreshing.

A few clouds had gathered in the sky, but Gray didn't need the moonlight for navigation. He knew this part of the woods well. Still, every so often, the moon peeked out and illuminated the trees and shrubs. Now that it was dark, the birds and other animals had gone to shelter, and the forest was silent. The only other movement was the silhouette of the dark-gray cat about fifty feet to Gray's left.

Gray didn't know if Brimstone was up to some mission of his own that coincidentally caused him to head in the same direction as Gray or if the cat was watching over him. He found the latter thought oddly comforting, though he wasn't sure how much help Brimstone would be if trouble arose. The cat had a reputation for saving his own hide first.

Gray had always loved being in the woods, especially at night. This was where he did his best thinking, and he had a lot of that to do if he wanted to clear his name. There was nothing like the cool air of a spring night with backlit clouds swirling around a sky of stars and being alone with his own thoughts.

As he crested a small hill, he realized he wasn't exactly alone. Two figures huddled on a massive fallen Scotch pine trunk ahead. Lovers?

But who would come this far into the woods just to neck?

He stopped, not wanting to interrupt the clandestine rendezvous. Was he still in the neutral section of the woods? Could it be a witch from the South Side meeting with a witch from the North Side?

A cloud drifted in front of the moon, turning the couple into dark shadows, but something familiar about them made him pause. He crept a little closer, using the thick woods as cover so the couple wouldn't notice him. Just as he made it alongside them, the moon slipped from behind a cloud, its silvery light bouncing off the pale face of none other than Stanley Judge.

Stan sat on the log, staring up into the sky with a dreamlike expression on his face. Ursula Lavoie snuggled alongside him. She glanced in Gray's direction. Gray held his breath and ducked behind a tree. Had Ursula seen him? He felt like a perverted peeping Tom.

Gray peeked back out. Ursula was still looking in his direction, a sly smile on her face, the moonlight sparking off her elongated fangs.

Gray backed up slowly. Whatever Ursula had going on with Stan was none of his business. In fact, more power to her. He didn't know what she saw in the guy, but maybe vampires liked those pasty types. Either way, getting Stan under her thrall would only serve to help the paranormal community. Because if Stan was part vampire himself and under Ursula's command, how could he possibly prosecute the rest of them?

Gray hurried back to his car. It felt awkward and dirty

to remain in the woods where Stan and Ursula were doing ... whatever it was they were doing. Funny, though, that Stan would be attracted to Ursula. Seemed like all kinds of couples from opposite sides were getting together. South Side and North Side witches, normals and paranormals, everyone was finding someone, no matter how big the obstacles. Everyone except him.

CHAPTER 13

The next morning Gray was up early, awaiting the text from DeeDee with the okay for him to return to the salon. Staying busy would hopefully distract him from everything else going on. He got ready, fed Cosmo, then headed for Issy's shop. He couldn't wait to tell her about Ursula and Stan, but he'd have to be careful not to reveal the reason he was in the woods. He didn't need his cousins knowing he had met with Starla Knight.

Glancing over at his shop, he saw the crime scene tape was still fluttering on the front door. No text from DeeDee yet. If he could just get inside to get his appointment book, he could at least start rescheduling his regulars. Plus, when he'd checked the salon's voicemail remotely, it had been full of messages from new people wanting to make appointments for the same style he'd given Mrs. Newcastle.

He chuckled and shook his head. Apparently he'd started some weird trend with the half-finished haircut he'd given her. Now if he could just get some replacement shears, he'd be all set.

Issy was busy behind the counter of Enchanted Pets when he arrived. Seemed she'd just gotten in a new shipment of solstice toads and was busy feeding the little purple buggers.

"Hey, cuz." He set Cosmo on an empty perch near the counter and went over to help nourish the hungry little amphibians. "You won't believe what I saw last night."

"What did you see? Oh, did you have any luck yet with the South Side witches?" Issy asked. "Bobby's the other suspect we need to question. I sure hope your plan works, whatever it is."

Good thing she was facing the opposite direction, because Gray just about swallowed his tongue. Which was silly, because there was no way anyone knew about his secret meeting with Starla in the woods the night before. They'd been careful, and he'd checked the area for spies. There'd been no one else around.

Issy slowly turned to face him, her expression suspicious. "Wait a minute. By that sheepish look on your face, I'm guessing you already talked to someone from over there, haven't you. Would her name be Starla?"

Gray waved his hand dismissively, trying to play off

the energy zooming through him like an Indy 500 car. "What difference does it make who it was? Besides, she helped us out once before, so I think she's our best bet."

"Uh huh." Issy's smile widened. "Is she a good bet for other things too?"

Heat prickled up Gray's neck from beneath the crew-neck collar of his black shirt. What he felt for Starla wasn't for public consumption. Not now. Maybe not ever. He scowled and turned away, more depressed by the forbidden nature of a relationship with Starla than he cared to admit. "No. And it wouldn't matter if she was. Our kind don't mix, remember? But speaking of that, I made a discovery last night about another couple who shouldn't mix."

Gray hoped the change of subject would keep Issy from further teasing about Starla. Normally his cousin's good-natured taunts never bothered him. But that was when they were about *other* women. Starla was ... different.

Issy looked up, a pinch of colorful wriggly rainbow worms for the toads poised above their terrarium. "Who?"

"Stan and Ursula."

Issy's brows shot up. "No kidding." She dropped the worms and peered in as one of the toads' tongues shot out, captured a worm, and sucked it back in practically faster than the eye could see. "What were they doing?

"They were sitting very close in the woods. *Very*

close." Gray reached into the terrarium and scratched one of the cute little toads on the head. It blinked up at him with bright-orange eyes.

Issy dusted worm goo off her fingers and closed the terrarium. "So there really is something going on between them?"

"It would appear that way," Gray said.

"That could be good for us. I mean, if Stan hooks up with Ursula, then he'll be on our side, just like Dex is." Issy patted him on the shoulder as she passed on her way to the register. "We'd have no worries about the FBPI."

"Yeah, but you know how it is. Normals and paranormals don't easily mix. It's bound to end in disaster." *Same as with South Side and North Side witches*, Gray thought.

"Well, that's what people said about me and Dex. Humans and witches don't belong together. Look at us now. We're very happy." She tilted her head. "And if it can work for us, maybe it can work for anyone who truly wants to be together. One shouldn't let a little thing like a relationship being forbidden stand in the way. Besides, it makes things more interesting that way."

Issy crossed her arms over her chest and plastered an innocent look on her face. He knew she was referring to him and Starla, but he didn't want to talk about that now. Better to steer the conversation in a more important direction, because if he didn't discover who had killed Eric soon, he would have a much bigger problem than his foundering love life. "You mean like Bobby and Beth."

"Sort of, although those weren't the two *exact* witches I was thinking of." Issy sighed, and her eyes softened. She must have sensed that she'd said enough and changed the subject. "You never did say if you found out anything more about Bobby and Beth."

"Not much, but Bobby Knight did have a true love back then, and he's been angry and bitter about it ever since," Gray said.

"Was it Beth? Why was he angry and bitter, because Charlie won her affections?"

"I don't think so. I mean, Charlie was married, and wouldn't everyone have noticed if he and Beth became an item?"

"You'd think Mrs. Stevens would have, at least."

Gray nodded. "And she wouldn't have been very happy about it, but back then, she was trying to prove Charlie didn't kill himself. Seems to me if she suspected him of cheating on her, she wouldn't have gone to the trouble."

"Good point. I still feel like this all ties back to Charlie."

"I agree. It's too much of a coincidence. With Charlie's barbershop being where my salon is and Eric being killed by my shears, there's gotta be a tie-in other than someone wanting to frame me."

"And another coincidence: Tim also had Eric working for him."

"That seems like an awful lot of coincidences, guys."

The sarcastic tones of Brimstone drifted down from the uppermost shelf of Issy's cat toy display.

"Cat's got a point," Issy said.

"Of course I do." Brimstone stretched, batted a fuzzy ball that dangled from one of the toys on the top shelf, and then jumped down from the display, landing with a soft thud before trotting to the back of the store.

"Don't you be getting into that new shipment of toads," Issy yelled after him.

"Me? I'd never do anything like that."

Issy rolled her eyes and started off after the cat. "Let's not forget about Beth lying. She's got to be mixed up in this, no matter how crazy her mind is."

"And Bobby Knight. He was angry when he left Eric's office. Could Beth be covering for Bobby?"

Gray came around the corner to see Brimstone standing on a step stool, one furry paw holding the top of the terrarium open.

"Hold it right there!" Issy yelled at the cat.

Brimstone turned innocent round, golden eyes on her. "What? I was just putting this little guy back. He lifted his other paw to reveal a purple toad that he was somehow holding in such a way so as not to harm it. "Dumb thing must've hopped out. Doesn't know a good thing when he has it."

Brimstone dropped the toad into the terrarium. "You should stay in there, buddy. Free room and board." He closed the lid before hopping on top of it and looking at

Issy. "You need to press down and make sure this thing is really secure so they don't get out."

"Umm, thanks for the tip," Issy said.

Brimstone hopped down and then walked off, swishing his tail in their direction. Just before he disappeared down the bird care aisle, he said, "You know, sometimes things aren't always what they look like. Sometimes it's exactly the opposite of what you think is going on."

Issy watched him go, her hands on her hips. "That cat. You never know what he's going to come out with."

"You can say that again." Gray thought about Brimstone's words as he watched his dark-gray tail disappear around the corner. Something clicked in his brain.

He snapped his fingers. "I got it! What if it was the opposite of what we've been thinking? What if it wasn't Beth who was lying about Eric?"

"What do you mean?"

"Beth said she was mad at Eric because he wouldn't take her case because he didn't work on anything to do with insurance. We knew she was lying because Tim had hired him to look into his mother's insurance claims. But what if Beth wasn't lying? What if Tim was lying about why he hired Eric? What if he really hired him to look into something with his father, and in doing so, Eric discovered something about what happened all those years ago?"

Issy stared at him for a few seconds and then started

toward the front of the store. "There's only one way to find out. We need to pay Tim Stevens another visit."

CHAPTER 14

Chocolates fresh from Ember's shop in hand, Gray and Issy arrived back on Tim Stevens's doorstep that afternoon. Gray had known they'd need an excuse to get in the door a second time and had remembered that Ember had mentioned Mrs. Stevens liked her vanilla creams. So what if they'd mixed a little truth potion in with the creamy vanilla centers? It was for a good reason. Spelling people without their consent was generally frowned upon in the paranormal community, but this was a special case. Gray was innocent, and he wasn't about to go to jail for a crime he didn't commit while the real killer roamed free.

Tim answered on Issy's second knock, his expression quickly morphing from wary to welcoming when he spotted the candy.

"Didn't think I'd see you two back here again so

soon," Tim said, letting them inside after a few seconds' hesitation. He seemed only mildly suspicious of their motives. Gray didn't know if that was good or bad. Judging by the questions they'd asked the other day, he'd have to be dense to not realize they were looking for Eric Naill's killer. If Tim was innocent, he wouldn't be suspicious. On the other hand, if he had killed Eric, he might *act as if* he wasn't suspicious to throw them off track.

"We wanted to do something nice for your mother after seeing her the other day. Ember mentioned she was fond of her vanilla creams." Issy took two boxes from Gray and handed them to Tim. One was the vanilla creams for his mother, the other peppermint bark, which Ember had said was Tim's favorite. "We also brought you some of your favorite peppermint bark too, to say thanks for answering our questions and for taking such good care of your mom."

Tim's cheeks flushed slightly as he took a seat on the sofa across from them. Today he was dressed in brown and nearly blended right into the room. "It's nice to feel appreciated."

"Yes, it is." Gray took a seat in an armchair beside Issy and glanced over to find Tim's mother out of bed today. She sat in a rocking chair near the unlit fireplace, knitting and mumbling to herself. Gray managed to pick out the words "barbershop" and "Charlie" from her otherwise unintelligible murmurs. "Perhaps your mom would like one of the vanilla creams now?"

"Here," Issy said, rising to take one to her. "Let me."

Tim's mother gobbled up the candy, her eyes immediately brightening and her foggy expression clearing thanks to the little spell Ember had cast over the treats. She picked up speed with her knitting. "Such a lovely day out, Timmy."

Gray glanced at Issy. That was the first semi-intelligible thing Mrs. Stevens had said. Apparently the chocolates were working.

Tim was surprised too. He looked at his mother wide-eyed. "What did you say, Mom?"

Her face clouded over. "Knit one, perl two. Or is it perl two and knit one?"

"I'm not sure, Mom." Tim's voice was full of hope that his mother would answer with something that made sense, but instead she fell back into the mumbling.

"Why don't we go in the kitchen," Gray suggested, nodding at Mrs. Stevens, who was fully absorbed in her knitting. It didn't look as if they were going to get anything out of Mrs. Stevens after all. He wanted to take Tim's focus away from his mother and figured he would be more willing to talk if he wasn't in the same room with her.

"Okay." Tim carried the box of peppermint bark with him. The kitchen was done in the same warm tones of brown and burnt orange. Most of the appliances looked as though they'd been transported from 1972, and the obligatory large wooden spoon and fork hung on the wall. They all took a seat around the small table near one side of the space, and Tim dug into his treats. Soon, he was grinning and bright, just like his mother in the other room. Except hopefully his words would make more sense.

"So Tim, I just found out that my hair salon is where your dad's barbershop used to be." Gray figured he'd warm Tim up, and then once he'd eaten enough candy, he'd hit him with the question about why he'd lied about hiring Eric. Plus, he wanted to see just how much Tim knew about his father.

"Yeah. That's where his shop was." Tim picked out another piece of peppermint bark and bit in.

"Do you remember much about the barbershop?" Gray asked.

Tim shook his head. "Nah, I was too young. Mom used to drive by and tell me about it, but it was empty then. No one wanted to rent it because of what happened to my dad."

"Tim. We know you lied to us about why you hired Eric."

Tim swallowed hard. He looked at Gray, then he looked at Issy, then he picked out another piece of bark and shoved it into his mouth.

"Eric didn't do insurance investigations. He wasn't looking into denied claims for you, was he, Tim? Can you tell us the real reason you hired a private investigator?" Gray persisted.

"Fine. I'm no good at lying anyway," Tim said, his posture slumping. "It was Mom. She wasn't always as senile as she is now. When I was younger, she was normal. Her mind got worse over time. One thing she's never forgotten is her belief that Dad didn't kill himself. She's always sworn it was murder. At first I was skeptical, but now I believe her. I don't remember much about my dad because I was so young when he died, but I do remember that he wouldn't leave us. There's no way he would have killed himself and left us unprotected like that. I wanted to prove it once and for all while my mom still had the capacity to understand what was happening. That's why I hired Eric. To dig into what really took place and reveal the truth."

"Even if it meant you found out your father was into something bad and that's what got him killed?"

Tim made a face. "My father was not into anything bad. Eric would have told us. He just said he was onto a good lead."

"And that's why you seemed so upset when we told you he was dead," Issy said.

Tim nodded, his eyes filling with tears as he reached for another piece of bark. "And now I'll never know who killed my father or be able to prove that my mother was right all this time."

Gray sat back and exhaled slowly. It seemed Tim wasn't the killer. He was too upset about not being able to prove the truth. Gray could see how desperate the guy was to prove that his father had not killed himself.

But Eric had told Tim he had a lead. It sounded like the investigation he'd hired Eric Naill to conduct had unwittingly opened a hornets' nest. One that someone clearly wanted closed up again. Then again, considering what Gray had heard about the black-market toad warts, that hornets' nest might reveal that Tim's father wasn't the upstanding citizen Tim thought. If word of his involvement got out, would that hurt Tim's mother even more? Tim seemed hell-bent on proving that his father didn't kill himself for his mother's sake. How far would he go to protect his father's reputation? Murder?

Then again, Eric would have never told Tim about the black-market toad warts because Tim wasn't a paranormal. Unless Charlie was into some illegal human stuff too, it was doubtful that Eric had given Tim information on his father that would cause Tim to want to silence him.

"I'd better check on my mom," Tim said and pushed to his feet.

Issy stood as well and followed him into the living room toward the front door. Gray heard their hushed tones and Issy saying, "Well, I think we've taken up enough of your time."

It seemed more and more that Eric's death was about that long-ago scandal. They still had no rock-solid evidence, but Gray would take his progress where he found it at this point. He stood and stretched then turned to go, only to find his path blocked by Tim's mother.

She grasped Gray's arm and stared up at him, her gaze earnest. "Charlie was a good barber. But he went off and never came home."

With a gnarled finger, she pointed to a photograph hanging on the wall beside the sink. Gray hadn't noticed it before, but upon closer inspection, he saw that it had been taken in Charlie's old barbershop, now his salon.

He recognized the big windows that looked out on Main Street and the black-and-white-checkered floor he'd liked so much. The floor looked shiny and perfect, not a tile out of place. Three barber chairs were lined up exactly where Gray had his stations. A crooked burlwood staff leaned against the back of one chair, and beside it stood a man who looked a bit like Tim — Charlie, Gray guessed. He had the long wizard hair, and the staff was a dead giveaway, because most wizards seemed to have one. Next to him was a younger version of Bobby Knight and a young woman. Beth Wilkins, maybe? The eyes were definitely the same. He'd been right; she had been beautiful.

"They were such good friends until things started to happen," Mrs. Stevens said. "A real barbershop quartet."

"Quartet?" Gray frowned and glanced back at Mrs. Stevens. "But there're only three people in this photo."

Tim's mother just shrugged and walked away, mumbling to herself, her expression going cloudy again as the candy in her system wore off. Weird. Usually Ember's spells worked better than that.

Frowning, Gray watched her go then glanced back at the photo. Charlie, Bobby, and Beth did look like good friends. In the photo, they smiled, not looking at all like three people involved in a love triangle that dealt in black-market toad warts.

He wondered if Mrs. Stevens knew about the love triangle her husband had allegedly been involved in. And was there a fourth person, or had that just been part of her rambling? Then again, maybe Mrs. Stevens was the fourth person taking a photo of her three friends before she found out her husband was a little friendlier with one of them than she'd thought.

CHAPTER 15

From Tim's house, Gray and Issy stopped by Raine's shop to discuss what had happened. On the way, he told Issy about his conversation with Mrs. Stevens in the kitchen and the photo.

"I wish you would've mentioned something before we left the house," Issy said as they walked into the tropical humidity of the Green Goddess. "I could've led Tim back there and asked him about it too."

Gray shook his head. "I don't think it would've done much good, though. Tim said he didn't remember much about his dad. He wouldn't have known who'd taken that photo. That was way before his time."

"Hey, guys," Raine announced, coming in from the greenhouse. "Ember told me she made some special chocolates for you to take to the Stevenses. How did that go?"

They filled her in on what had occurred.

"So it really wasn't Beth who lied about Eric, it was Tim?"

Gray nodded. "Yep. He didn't want anyone to know he had hired him to prove his father didn't kill himself. We got the truth out of him this morning, and while we were there, we saw the old photo of the barbershop."

"Interesting." Raine washed her hands and then dried them on a towel. "Just because someone took a picture of Beth, Bobby, and Charlie doesn't mean they were in on the black-market toad warts."

"True. But what if it was Mrs. Stevens and she found out about all the scandalous things going on?"

"Doesn't seem likely. She's not paranormal, so she wouldn't know about toad warts, and it doesn't seem she was very quick on the uptake if she didn't realize her husband was a wizard. Luigi said she never knew about that, right?" Raine picked up a small silver watering can and poured some water into the soil of Mortimer's pot. The Venus flytrap's leaves turned in Raine's direction to thank her.

"Good points," Gray said. "One thing is for certain: Eric's death has something to do with this whole business with Charlie. He was looking into the past and must have dug something up."

"Probably about the black-market toad warts. That's a much stronger reason to kill. Even now, if the council found out Beth or Bobby was involved, they would be fully punished," Issy said.

Gray rested his hips against a wooden work table and crossed his arms, thinking through all the facts they had so far. "I wonder if Mrs. Stevens was right all along about Charlie. He could have been killed because he found out either Beth or Bobby was selling the toad warts and threatened to expose them."

"True." Issy blew kisses to a butterfly that had landed on the back of her extended hand. "Beth and Bobby both hung around at the barbershop, and you said Tim's mother confirmed it from that photo in Tim's kitchen. And Gray told me Starla said Bobby never mentions what happened back then, so …" She waved her hand and the butterfly flew away. "Maybe he doesn't talk about it because he killed Charlie."

"You talked to Starla Knight?" Raine asked.

Gray winced. "Yes, but I don't want to discuss that right now, okay?" He did his best to keep his tone neutral and not defensive but failed miserably if the snicker he got from his cousins was any indication. He didn't miss their exchanged glances either.

"Of course you don't," Raine teased before dropping the subject. "But if you don't want to talk about that, then tell me about Stan and Ursula. Did you see anything juicy?"

"Not really. They were sitting pretty close." Gray

remembered the glint of Ursula's teeth. "Stan was pretty pale, and Ursula seemed ... err ... full."

"I knew it!" Raine's smile faded as she saw the tense look on Gray's face. "But that's not as important as getting to the bottom of Eric's murder. Now that we know more, we have to figure out who would have the most to lose if Eric revealed whatever it was he dug up."

"It would help if we knew what he dug up," Issy said.

"True, but we don't, so we need to think about who seems most guilty. My money is on Beth Wilkins. Her memory loss could be due to her guilt. It would explain why she's stuck in the past and can't remember," Raine said.

"I don't know. She didn't lie about why she argued with Eric. But it might be a good idea to talk to her again. She knew what went on back then." Gray pulled out his phone to check his calendar and saw the long-awaited message from DeeDee. The cops were finished at Shear Magic, meaning he could get back inside and begin cleaning up.

He had a lot to get done in there if he planned to reopen the following day. And he had his second meeting in the woods with Starla that night. The clock on his phone said three p.m. If they went to see Beth again at five, they should be done in plenty of time for his meeting with Starla, and no one would be the wiser. And because Beth liked to frequent happy hour at O'Hara's Pub, and it was close to Shear Magic, it was a win-win.

Granted, the bar wasn't the ideal place to question a suspect, but perhaps if she'd had a few drinks before they arrived, Beth Wilkins might be more amenable to talking to them. "How about five today at O'Hara's?"

"Works for me," Issy said. "If we can just get her to sort the real memories from the past and not mix them up with what's going on now, we might get the clue we need."

"How about we try a remembrance potion?" Raine suggested. "I've got the ashes of sage and dewdrops from a tiger lily. Issy, can you get me some ground up crow's nails?"

Issy nodded. "Just got a new shipment in the other day."

"Perfect!" Raine grinned, and for the first time Gray's own spirits lifted a bit. "I'll whip it up this afternoon, then we can slip it into her drink at the pub."

"Awesome." He started for the entrance. "I got word I can get back into my salon again, so I'm headed over there to start shaping things up for reopening. Let's plan to meet at the Main Squeeze first to coordinate it all. DeeDee usually stops there after work, and we can find out what the police have discovered before we talk to Beth."

CHAPTER 16

Gray went home to his cabin to pick up Cosmo before heading back downtown to Shear Magic. After unlocking the front door, he walked inside and surveyed the area. Cosmo flew around the room, checking everything out too.

Other than the things he'd spotted in disarray the day before, nothing else had changed. He checked the storage room in the back and found the cops hadn't made too big a mess there. There was some residue from the fingerprint dust on the back door, and counters and shelves too, but nothing some hard work wouldn't clean. He opened the back door to check the alley and froze. Martin Ellsworth was hunched over on the stoop, where he'd apparently been snooping around the lock again.

"Don't you have anywhere else to be?" Gray asked, his patience at an end.

Martin glared up at him and then straightened. "I could ask you the same thing."

"The police texted me. They're done with the investigation here." Gray squared his broad shoulders and crossed his muscular arms, doing his best to fill up as much space as possible to intimidate Martin. He didn't appreciate people snooping into his private business, and he'd endured more than enough of it already. "This is my shop. I'm free to be here and conduct business."

"And I'm free to conduct my own investigation into paranormal matters, per the Wizard Council." Martin looked completely unfazed by Gray's bravado, which was both irritating and worrisome. And Gray swore if he had to hear about that blasted Wizard Council once more, he could not be held responsible for his actions. "I'd be concerned about that if I were you, Graeme Quinn. Right now this investigation is pointing more and more toward you."

"Me?" Gray's confidence sagged a tad. "Why? What do you mean? I answered all Owen's questions, and they don't have any evidence I was involved at all, other than those shears."

Martin quirked a dark brow, his expression sly. "Perhaps they'd be interested in knowing about your clandestine meeting with the South Side. I hear you've been known to consort with them. Perhaps I should mention something to that fellow with the FBPI. What's his name? Stanley Judge. Yes. I'm sure he'd be plenty interested in your secret activities in the woods."

"What? That's ridiculous." Gray ran a hand through his hair. The last thing he needed was Stan sticking his nose further into this whole debacle. Then again, he now knew a few things about Stan that the FBPI agent might not want repeated, like his nightly rendezvous with their medical examiner.

Gray refused to show any sign of weakness around Martin Ellsworth. Wizards sensed fear, and the weasely ones like Martin preyed on it like carnivores. Gray wasn't interested in becoming anyone's dinner tonight. "Look, I'm trying to get to the bottom of this too. It's my butt on the line here, in case you haven't noticed. What about Bobby Knight? Have you checked into his involvement in all this?"

"What about him?" Martin's posture stiffened ever so slightly. Not enough that anyone else would've noticed, but Gray was studying the man closely. Defensiveness perhaps? The stubborn jut of the man's jaw made it difficult to tell. Bobby was a wizard, so maybe there was some tension between the two. Or maybe Martin was covering for his brother wizard. Maybe that was why he was so hot to pin this on Gray, so no one would investigate far enough to find out it was really Bobby. Whatever it was, Gray had hit a nerve. The knowledge pleased him. About time he got something right.

He continued to press. "I've got reason to believe that

Bobby Knight had something going on with Charlie Stevens here in what was the old barbershop. If Eric uncovered something about that during one of his investigations, that might have caused his death."

The rail-thin wizard quickly recovered, his dark eyes narrowed on Gray, glittering with spite. "I know all about that, and it has nothing to do with this. And the cases I investigate for the council are no one's business but my own. Besides, Charlie's dead. He could hardly have killed Eric Naill."

"No, but maybe Beth or Bobby did." Gray raised his chin, defiant. "Have you looked into them?"

"Are you insinuating I don't know how to do my job?"

Given that Martin was powerful enough to turn Gray into a lizard with one spell, he probably should've been more cautious, but he was tired and on edge and just wanted all of this to be over. He gave a slight shrug and stared at the brick wall across the alley. "Not insinuating anything. Just making a suggestion."

"Well, Graeme Quinn, here's a suggestion for *you*." Martin all but snarled the words, moving closer to poke his finger in Gray's face. "I'm collecting evidence and will soon have enough to take before the tribunal — maybe even as soon as tomorrow. If that police chief doesn't make an arrest by then, the tribunal will handle it. As I said before, I'd get my affairs in order if I were you, witch. How's that for a suggestion?"

CHAPTER 17

*A*mazing what a little outrage and terror could help accomplish. An hour after starting restoration work on his shop, Gray had the salon swept and dusted, most of his missed appointments rescheduled for a few days out when all this would hopefully be behind him and he'd have new shears from Switzerland, and all the supplies both in back and in front of the salon in order. He'd searched every nook and cranny, looking for something that might be a clue as to why Eric had been behind his shop and why someone had tried to unlock the door with magic, but found nothing. By the time he was ready to meet his cousins at the juice bar, he felt more determined than ever to prove his innocence.

"I can't believe he said that to you," Issy said half an hour later as she sipped her neon-fuchsia Berry Bliss. "So Martin was just lurking around behind your shop?"

"Yep, and yep. He said it, all right. Basically just came right out and told me that if Owen didn't have me arrested by tomorrow, he would have the council take me into custody." He shook his head and stirred the barely touched contents of his Purple Plum Passion. "It makes me ill thinking about it. I can't believe the guy's still building a case against me just out of convenience and spite, especially when I pointed out several much more viable candidates like Bobby and Beth."

"Either he is lazy, has a vendetta against you, or is covering for someone," Ember said.

"Hey, Quinn clan," DeeDee said, pulling up a chair. "What's this about Bobby and Beth?"

Gray filled her in on what he'd told Issy, Ember, and Raine. When he finished, he sighed. "Please tell me you have better news from Owen's end of things."

DeeDee sat back in her chair. "Well, we've looked into Bobby Knight. He doesn't have an alibi for the time of Eric's murder." At the Quinn cousins' collective gasp, she added, "But he doesn't have motive that I can find either. Sorry."

"How can you say that?" Gray scowled. "What about the scandal? The toad wart dealing?"

"Yes, but Owen doesn't know about that. And you don't have proof it was Bobby Knight doing the dealing. Until you can get me evidence, it's all just rumor and speculation. I need something that isn't paranormal to bring to Owen." DeeDee slumped. "My apologies, buddy, but you're still looking like the prime suspect at the moment, much as it pains me to say."

Gray's gut twisted with anxiety, and his blood pounded loud in his ears. "Wonderful. Now I've got not only Martin Ellsworth gunning for me but Owen too. I didn't do this. I swear I didn't. I need to find something to show I'm innocent."

"Hello, Quinn cousins," Luigi said, stopping by their table on the way to his pizza shop. "How are you holding up, Gray?"

Gray gave the chipper guy a flat stare. "How's it look like I'm holding up?"

"Yeah." Luigi snorted. "Ouch. I'm guessing you talked to Martin again. He's getting a lot of pressure from the higher-ups to get this case solved. I have to wonder, though, what the heck was Eric Naill doing at your shop anyway, Gray?" He toyed with his beard again, the way he always did when he was thinking. "Did you guys have some business to deal with in the middle of the night?"

"Of course not." Gray gave a long-suffering sigh. "I barely knew Eric. And I wasn't even there. I was at home. Alone."

"Hmm. Sure. Okay. Though it wouldn't be out of the ordinary for a fellow to have certain nightly meetings with people he shouldn't." Luigi narrowed his gaze on Gray, far too perceptive for his comfort. Did everyone in this infernal town insist on prying into his personal affairs? Luigi flashed a small, knowing smile and then shrugged. "And I'm already on the outs with the tribunal. I can't really afford to back the wrong guy here."

Gray glared at him across the table. Seemed nothing was private any longer, and everyone in Silver Hollow knew about him and Starla meeting in the woods. He'd been so careful, hadn't he? So, how in the heck was everyone finding out about his personal business? It grated more than he cared to admit. Even worse now that Luigi, the one ally he'd had on the tribunal, seemed to be wavering. Not good. Not good at all.

"I've caught Martin snooping around the back door of my shop twice now." Gray did his best to keep the bitterness from his tone, but he was well beyond the point of caring. "Obviously he thinks he's going to find some clue back there, though who knows what he's looking for. But if this is all tied to what happened with Charlie Stevens years ago, there very well might be something in the shop. But if there is, I have no idea where to look for it. I went through the entire shop today and didn't see anything odd."

Luigi frowned. "Did Martin mention anything about that to you either time you caught him lurking about your place?"

"Other than the fact he thinks I'm the killer? No."

"Interesting." Luigi shook his head and continued on his way to his pizza shop, muttering to himself as he went. Gray was coming to hate that word "interesting."

"It's five fifteen." Raine reached into the pocket of her

overalls and pulled out a little glass vial of glowing white truth potion. "Ready to talk to Beth?"

Thankfully, O'Hara's Pub wasn't as crowded as it usually was with the after-work crowd. Then again, it was still relatively early. A few regulars huddled around the bar, Beth among them. She smiled as Gray and the girls approached her.

"Did you bring me another plant?" Beth asked Raine. "That was lovely."

"Afraid not." Raine smiled. "We were going to get a booth. Care to join us?"

"Oh, well." Beth glanced at the people around her, already intoxicated, then nodded. "If you're sure you don't mind. It would be nice to have company."

Gray helped her off her stool and guided her to a secluded booth in the corner, where they could have maximum privacy. At the moment, Beth Wilkins seemed lucid and alert. They took seats in the booth — Issy and Raine on one side, Gray and Beth on the other — then each ordered drinks, beers for Gray and Beth, waters for Issy and Raine. Issy and Gray kept Beth occupied with gossip about other town residents while Raine slipped the potion into her beer. They all made small talk as Beth downed her drink. Luckily, it didn't take long.

Slowly, Gray steered the conversation toward the good old days. He found it odd that her memories only seemed muddled when it came to Bobby Knight and the barbershop. Otherwise she seemed to remember things as well as any Silver Hollow historian. She certainly seemed to remember their visit to her apartment the other day well enough. None of that seemed consistent with dementia, which seemed to be the prevailing theory of what was wrong with poor old Beth Wilkins.

"So, were you friends with Charlie Stevens back in the day?" Issy asked.

"Yes, I was." Beth smiled. "Charlie was such a nice guy. Where's he been, anyway? Haven't seen him in forever."

The cousins exchanged a glance.

"Do you mean Bobby Knight?" Raine leaned forward slightly. "You seemed really mad at him when we stopped by your place earlier."

Beth shook her head, and Gray looked past her out the window across the bar. There went Martin Ellsworth again, with Luigi following a few seconds later, both heading in the direction of his salon.

He clenched his fists, torn between wanting to charge out of the pub and demand to know what exactly Martin expected to find at his shop and grabbing hold of that long, swinging ponytail and giving it a good hard yank, just out of pure anger. And Luigi ... well, he obviously should've known better than to trust that guy. Those two were probably working together to gather evidence to convict Gray of a crime he didn't commit. Gray remembered how Luigi had asked him not to tell Martin that he'd visited his cabin. Was that because he was intending to work with Martin all along?

Beth moved, her arm knocking into his and jarring his attention back to the moment. Her expression had gone stormy the minute Raine had mentioned Bobby. She grumbled under her breath before answering. "He didn't even give me the time of day at Eric's office. And here I thought we were … we were …" She frowned, her eyes going glassy and confused. "What were we?"

"Is there anything else you can tell us about that day at Eric's office?" Gray asked, desperate. "Anything at all?"

"No. I'm sorry." Beth shoved her empty beer bottle away. "Excuse me a minute. I need to use the restroom."

They all watched her walk away.

"What's going on?" Gray hissed. "Your potion isn't working."

"The potion was fine. I made it correctly." Raine narrowed her gaze on the vial. "It's the same recipe I always use, and I've never had a problem in the past."

"I don't think it's the potion. She's not acting like someone with dementia would when taking this potion, but I think I know what the problem is," Issy said. "Beth isn't senile or crazy. She's been cursed to not remember anything associated with that time."

"But who would do such a thing?" Gray whispered, glancing around to make sure no one was listening. Normally he wouldn't be so paranoid, but circumstances being what they were, he couldn't be too careful. "And why?"

He glanced down at his watch. Dang! It was time to meet Starla. Talking to Beth had taken longer than he'd thought.

"Good question." Raine sat back. "Maybe it's —"

"Sorry, I need to go." Gray was already halfway to the door. "We'll talk more about this tomorrow. Thanks for your help today."

He jogged out of O'Hara's Pub, doing his best to stay positive and ignore the curious stares of his cousins burning a hole through his back.

As Gray walked into the woods, he couldn't help wondering who might have cursed Beth Wilkins. And if someone had cursed her, that probably ruled her out as the killer. Her reaction to the mention of Bobby Knight was making him more suspicious that the South Side witches had something to do with all of this.

The knot of tension between his shoulder blades tightened. He was on his way to meet Starla, and it wasn't much of a stretch to imagine this might be a trap. He whispered instructions to Cosmo to fly around and scope out the area to make sure there weren't any members of the South Side coven lurking about, waiting to ambush him.

Twilight had settled as he made his way through the trees toward the clearing at the center of the woods. Just before he reached it, Cosmo swooped back down onto his shoulder.

No one lurking about; just that pretty little finch, Starla, boss.

He entered the clearing and found her sitting on the log, alone. Cosmo flew to perch on a low-hanging branch while Gray approached her, feeling unsettled — both by the situation and by the woman herself. She was so pretty, like something out of a fantasy, and he could no longer deny the sparks of attraction that sizzled through him each time they were together, despite their precarious situation.

Starla looked worried too, her midnight blue eyes filled with concern. He didn't want to add to her burden and wondered if he should keep the information he'd learned so far from her. But he'd made a promise the night before, and he was a man of his word. Besides, being close enough to feel her warmth and smell her sweet perfume, it didn't feel like she was trying to screw him over at all. He sat beside her on the log and stared up at the starry sky, feeling a bit of his lingering tension from earlier drain away.

"Raine has a customer who was around back when the scandal happened. They said it had something to do with black-market toad warts." He hazarded a look at Starla, who glanced up sharply.

"Toad warts? I don't know anything about that," she

said. "Bobby wouldn't be involved in something like that."

"Issy and I went back over to Tim Stevens's place earlier. I saw a photograph Tim's mother had of Bobby, Beth Wilkins, and Charlie Stevens together at the barbershop back in the day. Issy thinks that Beth's been cursed. That's why she can't remember anything from that time." He exhaled and inched a bit closer to Starla just because it felt so darned good to be near her. "My instincts tell me something happened back then involving all of them, and I think your uncle Bobby might be the only one who knows the truth."

Starla sighed. "He still isn't saying much. He seems worried, scared. It's as if Uncle Bobby is afraid to talk for some reason. It's not like him to be afraid." She shook her head and stared out at the surrounding tree line.

"Did you find out what he was doing at Eric's office the day that Beth saw him storming out?"

"Bobby said Eric called him there. That's all he would tell me. He said it was nothing, that he was angry only because he didn't like having those old wounds reopened. He implied it was about the true love he lost."

Through the pale moonlight, Gray saw the sincerity on her beautiful face.

She shrugged. "When my Uncle Bobby was younger, he pushed the envelope. We all did. But he's older now, and he's a good man, I swear. When I mentioned Beth to him, he got this look on his face — heartbreak and happiness rolled into one. It was so sad." She sniffled. "My impression was that he was in love with her, but someone more powerful wanted her and forced them apart."

Gray thought about that. Was it Charlie? He was a wizard, and he did have that sturdy wizard staff Gray had seen in that old photo of the barber shop. Had Bobby killed Charlie out of desperation, to get Beth for himself, then covered up the murder as a suicide? That could certainly explain his fear. Killing a wizard was a big deal. But where did the black-market toad warts figure in?

"I know what you're thinking," Starla said at last. "I know, because I've been thinking the same thing: that Bobby killed Charlie to keep Beth." Her voice sounded strained. "Anyway, I went snooping around in his things to find something, anything, that might be a clue as to what really happened. Surprisingly, it wasn't hard to locate." She snorted. "Then again, maybe he wanted me to find it after all these years. It was in an old box, mixed in with old photos of Beth and the barbershop."

She reached into the pocket of her lavender dress and withdrew a large skeleton key. The iron glowed purple in the moonlight, a telltale sign of enchantment.

"What's it for?" Gray asked, staring at the thing.

"No idea."

"Huh. Well, whatever it's for, it could be used against your uncle."

Starla winced. "True. But it might also prove your

innocence. And as much as I love Bobby, if he did kill Eric, and possibly Charlie, then *he* should pay for his crimes, not you."

"You know, the killer used my magical golden shears to kill Eric." He wasn't sure why he was telling her, except that he needed to get it out, to share his fears with someone. "They're ruined now. So am I if I can't get another pair."

"What do you mean?" Starla frowned. "Gray, seriously. We might have grown up on different sides of town, but I remember how talented you were in high school. You made all the girls swoon with your hair styling. You didn't have those special scissors back then, and you did just fine. I'm guessing you'll do just fine now without them."

"But they were my secret weapon. I could use them to make any woman into exactly what she wanted."

"And you still can, using your abilities and the magic inside you." Starla smiled. "Don't doubt yourself, Gray. You're the most talented guy I've ever met."

She held the key out to him, and he reached for it, their fingers brushing. Gray leaned closer, unable to stop himself, as if drawn in by an invisible cord.

She believed in him even when he didn't believe in himself.

Starla inched nearer to him, her gorgeous midnight-blue eyes going all soft and dreamy. Only millimeters separated them now, her warm, minty breath fanning his face. His lips tingled with the urge to kiss her, to hold her, to find out if she tasted as sweet as she looked. A small niggle of warning echoed in his head — they shouldn't do this, they were too different, they were on opposing sides. Before he could capture her mouth with his, she turned and fled through the trees, leaving only a mumbled goodbye in her wake.

Gray stood for a long moment afterward, staring after her. Cosmo flew down to perch on his shoulder once more. He turned to head back toward the north side of town when a familiar voice echoed in the darkness.

"That was a close call," Brimstone said, trotting up beside him.

"What do you mean?" Gray said, weaving through the shadowed woods.

"You almost kissed her." Brimstone's feline tone dripped with disdain. "Seriously. What were you thinking? You need to learn to control yourself, man."

They emerged from the trees a few minutes later and headed toward Gray's car parked along the curb. Much as Gray hated to admit it, the nosy cat was right. He did need to control himself, at least around Starla, at least until this case was solved and his life returned to normal — no matter how tempting the thought of kissing her might be.

"So, what did she give you?" Brimstone asked, breaking him out of his thoughts.

"This." Gray showed him the key.

"And what does it open?"

"No clue. That's the problem. Starla seemed to think it might reveal the truth about what happened way back then and could help me figure out who killed Eric."

"Is that what you think?" Brimstone purred before stopping to groom some strands of orange cat fur from his tail.

"Not sure, but it's the only lead I've got." Gray unlocked his car and then opened the driver's-side door. "Too bad there's no way to know what it unlocks."

CHAPTER 19

Gray spent a sleepless night wondering about the key that Starla had given him. There was no guarantee that key was even related to Eric's murder or to any of the events surrounding the barbershop long ago. Then again, there was no guarantee that the events surrounding the barbershop had anything to do with Eric's murder.

Deep down, Gray knew they were all related and that the key was significant. Starla must've also felt that way; otherwise she wouldn't have given him the key — unless she wanted to throw him off track. If she was working with her uncle Bobby, it could all be a clever smokescreen to get him to focus his attentions on someone else.

Even if she wasn't working with Bobby, Bobby could have known that they were meeting and planted the key for Starla to discover. She'd said it wasn't difficult to find a box of old photos or the key that was in it.

Could it be a trap? But how? Gray couldn't worry about that now. He had to try to find out what the key opened.

When he'd emerged from the neutral woods the night before, his phone had lit up with concerned texts from his cousins. He'd replied to each, assuring them that he had a good reason for his abrupt departure and informing them there was a new clue to discuss. They'd agreed to meet first thing in the morning at the juice bar, and that was where Gray headed after dropping Cosmo off at his shop.

The days were getting warmer now, and the early-morning sunshine was evaporating the last of the dew on the grass in the commons when Gray arrived at the bar to the sounds of chirping birds.

His cousins were already sitting at a table with glasses of colorful juice in front of them and inquisitive frowns on their faces.

"Where did you go last night?" Issy asked as she shoved an electric-blue drink in front of him. A Tropical Treatise? Or was it a Tremulous Typhoon? Gray couldn't remember the names of all the drinks.

"Yeah, what was the big emergency?" Raine asked.

"I had a meeting that turned out to be very fruitful." Gray slurped the drink. Coconut mixed with a breezy hint of seashore. Delicious.

"With who?" Ember's eyes narrowed. "Wait a minute, I can guess who …"

Gray didn't want his cousins to speculate about what went on in the meeting, so he pulled the key out of his pocket and placed it in the middle of the table. It sparked purple and then sat there glinting in the sun. To any regular human passing by, it would look like a plain old skeleton key. The enchantment was only visible to paranormals.

Gray glanced toward the pizza window to make sure Luigi couldn't see the key. If Luigi was working with Martin Ellsworth, Gray didn't want to tip his hand about what clues he was pursuing. The window was dark. It was too early for pizza, and Luigi wasn't here yet.

"Where did you get that?" Ember asked.

"Starla Knight." Gray ignored the knowing glances his cousins gave each other. "She got it from Bobby. I think it has something to do with everything that happened concerning the toad warts and Charlie Stevens."

"Really?" Issy picked the key up and hefted it in her palm. "What does it open?"

Gray sighed and slumped back in his chair. "I wish I knew."

"That kind of key could open anything. An old box. A hidden compartment. It could be in someone's house, in their car, or buried in their backyard. How will we ever figure out what it opens?" Raine asked.

"I guess we need to use good old-fashioned detective

work. If there was some evidence on the black-market toad warts, it makes sense that someone would hide it and enchant the hiding place." Issy put the key back in the center of the table. "Trouble is that since it's enchanted, the hiding spot might not be easy to find."

Ember frowned. "Yeah, but if it was Bobby Knight, wouldn't he have the box or whatever this key opens in his possession? How will we find it if it's in his house or his car?"

"He might have it, but it would be smarter to give it to someone who was close so he wouldn't be caught with it. Someone like Beth Wilkins," Issy said. "We know someone cast a spell on her to forget things. Maybe it was Bobby. He wanted her to forget where he'd hidden the evidence because it points to him."

"Sounds like a good plan. We need to talk to Beth again to see if we can look around her house." Raine whipped out her cell phone and started thumbing something in. "We exchanged numbers last night because she wants another one of those plants we brought over to her place."

"That's a great place to start." Issy also started thumbing a text. "Another place we need to look is the Stevenses' house. I just got in some really cool aquarium decorations. We can use them as an excuse to go to Tim's."

"So what do you think this hidden evidence is?" Ember asked.

Gray shrugged. "I don't know. Old dried up toad warts? Paperwork, like bills of sale for toad warts. Who knows?"

"It might have something to do with Charlie Stevens's death," Issy said. "Maybe some evidence that he didn't kill himself."

"Or it could be nothing at all," Gray added. He didn't want to get his cousins' hopes up. He had to admit he was relying on this one a little bit more than he liked, but with no other clues to follow, what else could he do?

Raine's phone dinged. "Beth's at the applesauce factory taking some test to see if she can go back to work, but she said to stop by her place around one. Does that work for you guys?"

"I could make that work. I have to go open up the shop this morning, but I can have Hannah watch it this afternoon," Issy said.

"Works for me," Ember said. "I'll make Beth some relaxing chocolates so that she doesn't notice us poking around her place too much."

"I'm pretty much free all day. I don't have clients coming in for a few days," Gray said.

"Great. I'll let her know." As Raine thumbed in her response, Issy's phone dinged.

"Tim says he's taking his mom for some tests in Epping, and he won't be home till around five tonight. Actually, that works for me. I have some things to do after we get back from Beth's, but I can close up the shop a little early so we can head over."

"Yeah, that could work for me too." Ember pushed up from the table. "Speaking of which, I'd better get to my shop if I'm gonna get those chocolates made. I'll make extra for Tim and his mom."

Raine tossed her cup into the trash and stood. "Yep, me too. I'll pick everyone up at quarter to one, and we'll head to Beth's."

"Hold up, Raine. I'll walk with you. I'm getting a delivery in fifteen minutes." She threw her cup in the trash, then looked back at the table. "See you at one, Gray."

"See you then." Gray scooped the key off the table and put it in his pocket as he watched his cousins walk off. He didn't have customers coming in today and was in no hurry, but he could still make sure the shop was in order. He was nervous about reopening and wanted to make sure everything was exactly where he wanted it to be.

He took the last sip of his drink, stood up, and turned, practically running smack into Owen, Dex, and Stan.

OWEN HELD his hands up in front of him. "Whoa, where you running off to?"

"I was done with my drink, so I was going to my shop." Gray didn't like the way the three of them eyed him, as if they had come here just for him. Was he being arrested? His eyes flicked to Dex, but Dex had his poker face on, and his expression held no hint as to why the three of them stood there as though they wouldn't allow Gray to pass.

"What's up? You guys here for juice? The Tropical Tornado is really good today." He held up his empty cup, the blue foam still bright at the bottom, and gave Owen a fake smile that he hoped would convey he wasn't nervous at all about running into them.

"Oh, that's good, real good." Owen's eyes flicked toward the juice bar. "I was looking for you, though. Maybe I'll have one after."

Shoot! Gray had to do something to stall. He couldn't get arrested now. Not before he had a chance to figure out what the key opened. "Oh? I'm kind of in a hurry to set up shop. You know, you guys did kinda leave it in a bit of a mess."

Owen frowned. "We did? I instructed the guys to make sure it was left exactly as they found it."

Maybe Gray shouldn't have said that. It wouldn't be smart to anger Owen right now. "Well, it wasn't that bad. But you know me, I'm particular."

"Yeah, that's kinda what I wanted to talk to you about. See, I was wondering about those shears of yours. I still don't understand how they could've gotten outside of your shop, you know, with you being so particular and all."

"I've been thinking about that, too. It was really busy that day in the shop. I mean, it's possible someone lifted those scissors when I was cleaning up after the haircuts." Not exactly a lie. Gray was sure someone had lifted the scissors after he was done, but not exactly in the way he implied. But Owen didn't understand about magic, so this was the nonmagical equivalent of what had really happened.

Gray glanced at Stan. He was just standing there, pale as ever, his lips looking bloodless. He kept glancing uncomfortably over his shoulder at the sun. He wasn't really paying that much attention to Gray, which was good. Normally Stan would focus his beady gaze on Gray as if he was a bug under a microscope, but now he was more interested in the blazing ball in the sky. Gray made a mental note to buy Ursula a juice the next time he saw her. He owed her one.

"You don't say?" Owen rocked back and forth on his sneakered heels. "I thought you said before that you'd notice right off if someone took them while the shop was open."

"I thought I would, but maybe I got busy ..." Gray glanced at Dex for help.

"Yeah, if someone wanted to frame you, that would be the time to do it: the end of the day when there's been a run and you don't have any more haircuts scheduled," Dex said.

Owen stroked his chin. "I could see that. So who was in your shop that afternoon?"

"Well, I wasn't exactly keeping track. I mean, there were the ladies I had just given haircuts, of course. Sometimes they sit around gabbing for a bit, but I don't think any of them would've killed Eric."

"Can you get me a list of who had haircuts that afternoon?" Owen asked.

Crap! Gray didn't want to give Owen a list of his customers so they could be harassed by the police. But he had to stall, because he needed time to investigate the key.

"Sure. I'd have to get back to my shop and look through the appointment book."

Stan darted over to a nearby table, pulled a chair out, and sat under the shade of the umbrella. "I don't see what all this is going to get us. I don't think the little old lady who was having a haircut would've murdered a young man like Eric Naill. Maybe I should go to the morgue and double check that an old lady would've had the strength to stab him like that."

"Huh, that's a good idea, Stan," Owen said.

"Yeah. You seem to have developed a rapport with our medical examiner, so you should go." Dex's lips twitched, trying to suppress a smile.

"Okay, I'll meet you guys back at the station." Stan

shot up from the chair and bee-lined for the shade of a tall oak tree, then made his way toward the public offices while keeping to the shaded side of the street.

"What do you think is wrong with him?" Owen asked Dex. "I mean, if he needs some sunscreen, I have some at the office. I think a little bit of sun would do him good. He's pale as a ghost."

"Right. Well, if that's all, I'll be getting to my shop now so I can get you that list." Gray edged away from Owen.

"What? Oh, okay. Sure. I got to get me one of those Tropical Tornados. Talk to you later." Owen headed toward the juice bar.

Dex hung back, waiting for Owen to get far enough away before leaning over toward Gray. "Issy said you guys are working on a lead. I'll try to stall Owen long enough for you to work it through, but I have to warn you, he really wants to make an arrest soon." Dex slapped him on the shoulder and started off to join Owen. "Better work fast, buddy," he called over his shoulder.

Gray tossed his cup in the trash and trudged toward the salon, his spirit sinking. He shoved his hands in his pockets, his fist curled so tightly around the key that it dug painfully into his palm. He needed to make sure nothing happened to it. That key might be a longshot, but right now, it was his only shot.

Gray spent the next several hours puttering around in his salon and trying to keep his anxiety at bay. He trusted Dex to distract Owen, but how long would that work? Eventually Owen would want to make an arrest, and if the evidence pointed to Gray, he didn't think there was much Dex could do about it.

Which was why he desperately needed to figure out what the enchanted key unlocked. It had to be something important, because no one enchanted a key to hide unimportant things.

His hand stole into his pocket again to reassure himself the key was still there. Hopefully this would be the thing that got him off the hook, because if not, he didn't really have any other better ideas.

I can spy on that Bobby Knight dude, boss man, Cosmo

telepathed from his perch where he'd been watching Gray obsessively clean the same spot repeatedly.

"Nope. Too dangerous, buddy." Maybe if they lived in the tropics where cockatoos flew around in the wild, it would be okay, but Cosmo flying around the South Side looking for Bobby Knight would be dangerous. It wasn't as though the South Side witches didn't know that Gray had a cockatoo for a familiar. That was too dangerous, and he didn't want Cosmo to get hurt because of him. But maybe there *was* something Cosmo could do for him.

"You can come to Beth's and help search." With his keen eyesight and ability to fly, Cosmo could search the place much faster than any human. Gray pulled the key from his pocket, holding it flat in his palm. "Look for any kind of box that this might open."

Cosmo ruffled his wings. *Not just a box. Enchanted keys can open anything.*

"Right. Good point." Gray made a mental note not to focus too much on boxes and to check the walls, floors, even the ceiling tiles for hidden compartments. Heck, even boxes could have hidden compartments, and he shouldn't overlook books, which could be hollowed out, or even kitchen canisters that could have false bottoms. The possibilities were endless.

Don't worry. I know what to look for. Cosmo preened the feathers under his right wing.

At twelve forty-five, Raine's yellow Jeep pulled up in front of his shop. The top was down, and his three cousins were inside. Gray hopped in with Cosmo on his shoulder. The bird immediately flew to the roll bar, clutched his massive claws around it and squawked, *"Let's go!"*

Issy turned in the passenger seat and looked at Gray over the top of her sunglasses. "How are you doing? I heard you ran into Owen and Dex."

Gray nodded. "And Stan. But he seemed more interested in finding an excuse to hang around at the morgue."

Raine snorted as she pulled away from the curb then glanced at him in the rearview mirror. "It's great that Stan is too interested in Ursula to think about capturing you, but how are you going to persuade Owen to drop you as a suspect?"

"I'm not worried. Hopefully we'll find something at Beth's, and we can get DeeDee to help us integrate that into the investigation." Gray tried to act nonchalant. He didn't want his cousins to know how worried he actually was, but judging by the glances they all gave each other, he wasn't fooling anyone.

Issy turned back around to face front. "Dex will hold them off as long as he can. We have to work fast. If we don't find anything at Beth's, we need to get to Tim Stevens's place at five o'clock sharp."

They drove the rest of the way in silence, except for Cosmo, who squawked while his head bobbed up and down, his neck craned forward to catch the breeze. Gray was always a little worried that the wind would rip Cosmo from the roll bar when they drove in Raine's Jeep, but the bird seemed to love it and always managed to keep his grip.

Gray wasn't sure why he worried. After all, Cosmo could fly.

Beth seemed happy to see them and even happier to see the oversized plant Raine had brought. She invited them in and then sat on the sofa, putting the plant on the coffee table in front of her, stroking its leaves lovingly. "Hey, thanks for drinks the other night." Beth sank back into the couch. "We did have drinks, right? My memory is a little fuzzy."

Raine sat down next to her. "Yeah, it was fun to get together." She pushed the plant a little closer to Beth, who sighed and closed her eyes.

Cosmo took the hint and flew off into the kitchen, making a slow circle around the room, checking for secret compartments. He landed on the countertop, his beak tapping on the canisters.

Issy, Raine, and Ember kept Beth talking. The plant had relaxed her enough so that she was practically asleep. Once Gray was convinced she wasn't paying attention to him at all, he conducted his own search, starting in the bathroom, which was a total bust. Beth didn't have much clutter, and even the linen closet was mostly empty, with only five towels and three washcloths. No boxes or secret compartments.

In the bedroom, he found a jewelry box, but the key didn't fit. He held the key in his palm, figuring it would light up if it was near the item that it unlocked. He made a circuit around the room, going into the closet and pushing the key under the bed, but it never sparked, and he found no boxes or hidden panels.

I got nothing. You get anything? Cosmo asked.

"Nope." Gray went back into the living room, where his cousins were still talking to Beth.

"I don't know why my memory is so inconsistent. Sometimes it seems like I remember things fine, but other times it's almost like a veil is in front of me when I try to remember. Especially back years ago when I was younger."

Raine looked up and caught Gray's eye. Further proof that Beth had been cursed.

"But you remember some things. And I bet you have some keepsakes from back then." Issy glanced over her shoulder at Gray, frowning when he shook his head to indicate he hadn't found anything. "Like maybe some keepsake boxes with mementos?"

Beth frowned. "I don't have anything like that. As you can see, I live a very simple lifestyle. I don't like clutter or knickknacks."

"But you remember Charlie and Bobby, right?" Ember asked.

A smile played on Beth's lips. "They were very nice."

"The three of you were pretty close, weren't you?" Raine asked.

Beth frowned. "I think so. But Bobby doesn't talk to me anymore, and Charlie ... well, he's gone."

"What about Charlie's wife? Did you know her very well? She must've been part of your group." Gray still wasn't sure if Eric had stumbled upon information about a love triangle or the toad warts.

"Oh yes, she was very nice. I didn't really know her that well. She didn't come around the barbershop that much, but she was funny," Beth said.

"Did they have a good marriage?" Issy asked.

"Yes, I think so." Beth smiled. "And they had that adorable kid. Tim. Of course he's all grown up now. Looks like Charlie."

Judging by Beth's fond memories, it didn't seem she'd had a secret relationship with Charlie. So maybe Eric's discovery did have to do with the black-market toad warts and not some clandestine affair. Which meant that Tim Stevens wouldn't have had a reason to kill Eric so as not to bring the affair to light.

"But something happened at the barbershop, didn't it?" Raine asked.

Beth's face clouded over. "Yes. Charlie died."

"No, before that. Something to do with the toads."

Beth made a face. "Toads? I don't know anything about toads. I only know we used to hang around there, and then Charlie died and the shop was closed."

Raine glanced up at Gray, the expression on her face asking if he was done looking. Gray nodded. He hadn't found anything, and the conversation was going nowhere. Looked like their trip to Beth's had been a bust.

The cousins said their good-byes and got back into Raine's Jeep. As Gray slid into the back seat, he felt a dark cloud settling over him. They hadn't found anything at Beth's that could help clear his name, and he was rapidly running out of both time and options.

CHAPTER 21

Raine dropped Gray and Issy off in front of Issy's pet store. They all had to get back to their businesses for the afternoon but agreed to meet at Issy's again just before five so they could go to Tim Stevens's home.

Gray and Issy parted ways, and he crossed the street on the way to his shop, the key tucked firmly in his pocket and Cosmo perched lightly on his shoulder.

He was almost to his front door when a figure emerged from the alley, blocking his way.

Martin Ellsworth.

Gray glanced down the alley in time to see the flap of a long coat disappear around the corner. Luigi? Had he been meeting with Martin and passing him information about Gray? Were they following him?

"I heard you and your cousins paid a visit to Beth Wilkins today." Martin looked at him as if he were a fly that had dropped into his French onion soup.

News traveled fast in the town. "Yeah, so? She's a friend."

"Really? Or would you be meddling in an important investigation?" Martin's eyes narrowed and flicked over to Issy's shop. "You wouldn't want your pretty little cousins to be arrested for obstructing wizard justice, would you?"

Gray's heart lurched. Was Martin threatening his cousins? "What do you mean? Like I said, we went to visit a friend."

"I know what you're up to, Mr. Quinn. And I know what you've done."

Cosmo dug his claws into Gray's shoulder and telepathed an image of him pecking Martin. Gray telepathed back the word *no*. Familiars that harmed other paranormals, especially powerful wizards, usually met with a very unfortunate fate.

"That's the thing. I'm not *up to* anything. But it seems as if someone is trying to make it seem that I am. Someone is trying to frame me, and because no one will believe me, I have to figure out who the real killer is on my own."

Martin stepped a little closer, and Gray got a whiff of foul wizard's breath. It smelled like rotten quail eggs mixed with decades of mildew. "It's not gonna help you anyway. I'm very close to putting the final nail in your coffin. All I need is one little piece of evidence. Just another day or so, and you'll be done."

Martin stepped back and stabbed the end of his staff in Gray's direction. "And you'd better stop investigating unless you want to see those innocent little cousins of yours in paranormal jail."

And with that Martin whirled around and disappeared back into the alley.

Bad man, Cosmo telegraphed.

"You can say that again." Gray glanced over at Issy's shop. She stood at the counter, smiling at a customer who was buying a small green gecko. The gecko reminded him of the one she'd given to Dex. Which reminded him about how happy she was now that she'd found Dex. He couldn't do anything to jeopardize her happiness or that of his other cousins. If having them help him would get them into trouble, then Gray needed them to stop.

And if Gray didn't figure out who killed Eric soon, he wouldn't be around to protect them in the future.

The key burned hot in his hand. There was only one thing left to do. He had to use the key to reveal whatever it was that Bobby Knight had hidden. Only then would he have the evidence to clear himself.

If the box was in Bobby Knight's possession, then Gray was out of luck. And the only other place it could be was Charlie Stevens's house. Tim and his mother wouldn't be home for hours.

But Gray couldn't wait for hours. He turned on his heel and headed toward his car. He needed to conduct a thorough search of the Stevenses' house now.

CHAPTER 22

Breaking and entering by magic was frowned upon in Silver Hollow, but Gray didn't have much choice. Still, he felt like a thief as he stood in front of the Stevenses' back door, flexing his long fingers over the locked door knob.

"Apertania inalasorous!"

Click.

A puff of purple dust flew out of the keyhole. The air filled with the smell of melting wax, and the door popped open.

Gray stepped inside.

The house was so quiet that Gray heard his heart beating. The anticipation of getting caught had quickened his pulse, but he willed himself to calm down. He needed to conduct a methodical search, and Tim and his mother would not be home for hours.

Besides, it wasn't as though he was some common thief that was going to rip them off. Well, okay, he would take something if it would prove his innocence, but it probably wouldn't be anything that Tim or his mother would even realize they had. Now if only he could figure out where Charlie might've hidden it — whatever "it" was.

He took a deep, cleansing breath. He still felt as if he was violating the Stevenses, but Martin's threatening words against his cousins gave him the bravery to continue.

I'll check the bedroom down the hall. Cosmo flew off, and Gray started in the living room.

He wasn't even sure what he was looking for. An old box full of things from Charlie's barbershop? Or maybe Charlie Stevens had some sort of secret hiding spot. He lifted the rugs, looking for a loose floorboard, tapped on the walls, and covered every inch of the cabinets. He looked inside the entertainment center and the china closet and even between the mattresses.

But he found nothing.

He took the key out and passed it over every surface. It never sparked.

Cosmo didn't have any luck either.

When they finally met in the kitchen, Gray was crawling on his hands and knees, looking inside the bottom cabinets, desperate to find something hidden in the back.

"Dammit!" Gray crawled out of the cabinet and sat in the kitchen chair, his heart heavy.

Nothing? Cosmo perched on the kitchen counter, the crest atop his head sticking straight up.

"Not a thing. Maybe this was all a wild goose chase. It makes sense that if Bobby had the key, then Bobby probably has the box, or maybe he has it hidden in a secret compartment somewhere at his place." Gray's spirits plummeted. There was no way he could look through Bobby's house. Could he talk Starla into doing it? What if she got caught? Would Bobby harm her? The thought made Gray's heart squeeze painfully. He couldn't ask her; it was too dangerous.

Gray looked around the kitchen one last time, his eyes coming to rest on the photo that Tim's mother had shown him from the barbershop with Beth, Bobby, and Charlie all smiling.

The photograph had been taken three decades ago, but the shop looked so familiar because Gray had kept so many of the original features. Looking at it almost made him cry. He loved the shop. He loved styling hair. He loved his life here in Silver Hollow. And now he was going to lose it all.

He thought about how he'd painstakingly restored the barbershop to maintain the retro look. He'd even bought vintage glass doorknobs and repaired the crown molding. Not everything was the same, though. Gray didn't have the old-fashioned barber chairs, and he'd brought in shelving for his hair products. But the rest of it was the same, right down to the black and white tile flooring.

Except for one thing. The tile in the photo was perfect. But when Gray had moved in, there was one section where two black tiles had been placed together. It had always bugged him that whoever fixed the floor hadn't taken the time to use the right tile, and he'd never been able to find those exact tiles so he could fix it himself. It had bothered him so much that he'd put one of the display shelves on top so he didn't have to look at it.

And then something clicked.

Gray had to get back to his shop right away.

Gray rushed out of the Stevens house to find Brimstone on the hood of his car.

"Get in, I'm in a hurry," Gray commanded.

"Yeah, I know. I'm a familiar, remember?" Brimstone replied as he hopped in the open driver's-side door. "I sensed the urgency and figured I'd come to help you."

Interesting. The cat talked a good line but was always there whenever they needed help the most.

As Gray made his way back to the salon, he half expected to see Martin and Luigi run out into the road to flag him down and haul him off to see the tribunal on some trumped-up charges. Still, with Brimstone purring on the passenger seat beside him and Cosmo perched on the back of the rear seat, his mind wandered over the facts of the case and what the key might open. The whole thing could be just another ruse or trap to throw him off the scent of the real killer.

"Why was Eric at my shop to begin with?" Gray mused aloud.

"If that key of yours unlocks something in the salon, it makes sense," Brimstone said.

Cosmo squawked a telepathic response. *Who else knew there'd be something hidden in there?*

"Bobby, of course," Gray said. "It's his key."

He turned the corner to head around the town square. "Charlie was selling illegal toad warts, or at least someone was. Charlie, Beth, and Bobby were close friends. And Martin Ellsworth investigated the case back then, but Charlie killed himself before he could be prosecuted."

"What if Charlie wasn't the one dealing in toad warts?" Brimstone asked.

What if Martin was about to discover it was actually Bobby Knight who was selling the warts and Bobby did something to frame Charlie? Cosmo suggested.

"Good point." Gray pulled into his usual parking spot in front of his shop. "Maybe Beth knew too. They were all close. Bobby could have cursed her so she wouldn't remember the details. That would explain why Bobby was so angry when he left Eric's office."

"And that could also explain why Martin Ellsworth is so hot on your case now," Brimstone added. "Because everyone knows he was gunning for the wrong man back then. He needs to redeem himself. And Bobby could have killed Eric, especially if Eric was asking about that old case and Bobby feared he was getting too close to the truth."

Gray hefted the key in his hand. "Well, if my hunch about what this unlocks is correct, we may be about to discover what really happened back then."

As they walked up to the entrance of Shear Magic, something still didn't sit right with Gray. He thought back to the old photo he'd seen hanging in the Stevenses' kitchen. Tim's mother had said the four of them were friends, but only Beth, Charlie, and Bobby were in the photo. He'd never found out who the fourth member of their group was. At first he'd thought it was Mrs. Stevens, but Beth had said she didn't come to the barbershop much.

Gray unlocked the front door and rushed inside, Brimstone and Cosmo right behind him. He rushed to the shelf unit he'd positioned to hide the mismatched tile and moved it aside before crouching down.

Brimstone padded to him and sniffed the area before backing away. "Something stinks."

He didn't smell anything, but Gray didn't have heightened feline senses. "What does it smell like?"

"Betrayal." Brimstone's eerie orange eyes glowed in the darkness.

As he removed the key from his pocket, Gray's mind

whirled. Someone was betrayed back then. Was it Charlie? Bobby? Beth? All three of them?

Cosmo landed on Gray's shoulder, and they all stared down at the mismatched tiles as he held the key over them. The key glowed bright purple. Magic pulsed through the air, and a sharp click sounded. The tiles slid open, and the stench of rotting toad warts wafted out. Gray's pulse stumbled. Inside was evidence that proved someone had been selling black-market toad warts.

The photos from the Stevens's kitchen flashed into his mind again. The three friends stood there, but there'd been something else — a burlwood staff leaning against the back of one of the chairs. Gray's stomach swooped as he realized that staff hadn't belonged to Charlie, it belonged to the fourth member of their group, the person who'd taken the photo. Tim's mother had said they were all good friends. They'd all looked so happy in the photo before things went bad. Before one of them betrayed them all.

Martin Ellsworth.

He'd been at the heart of things both now and then. When Beth claimed she saw him at the barbershop, Gray had thought she'd meant she'd seen Martin investigating Eric's murder and just got confused between the past when it had been a barbershop and its present function as Gray's hair salon.

But what if she'd really meant she'd seen Martin the night Charlie died? What if Martin was dealing in black-market toad warts and he'd framed Charlie Stevens, and Beth was a witness? Martin was certainly a powerful enough wizard to curse her into forgetfulness. And he had a crooked burlwood staff, just like the one in the photograph.

If his suspicions were true, then Gray needed to get the smelly mess out of his floor and get it to the proper authorities right away. He reached into the hole in the tiles and found not a package of slimy warts, as he'd expected, but instead a crinkled old scroll. He'd just started to pull them out when a voice spoke from behind him.

"I see you found those documents. That's good for me … and bad for you."

CHAPTER 24

Cosmo shrieked and flapped his wings. Brimstone hissed, "Oh crap!"

Gray turned to find Martin Ellsworth standing behind him, his crooked burlwood staff pointed directly at Gray's heart. How he'd gotten in without any of them hearing Gray didn't know, but it hardly mattered now. He moved slowly, his hands up to show he wasn't a threat.

As if in answer to his thoughts, Martin said, "An audio cloaking spell. I suspected you were meeting with the little witch from the South Side. If only you hadn't been so quick to figure it out. All I needed was another day to have you arrested by the human authorities. You could have spent the rest of your life in prison. Now I'll have to silence you. Permanently."

Straightening, Gray took stock of the items around him — hairspray, bottles of shampoo and conditioner, dryers and combs and brushes. Nothing he could use as a weapon. He needed to stall for time, maybe get Martin talking some more. "You killed Eric Naill."

Martin shrugged as if he'd mailed the wrong letter, not taken a life. "Had to. He would have discovered the truth, and I couldn't have that."

If he could just make it to his station, he could grab one of the pairs of scissors he had lined up on the counter. "Did you also kill Charlie Stevens?"

"Same situation," Martin said, his tone bored. "He was going to reveal my little side business."

"The toad warts?" Gray said, inching toward his station.

With a nod, Martin glanced down at the floor, where the tiles were sliding back into position. "He said he had proof. I never found it. Then again, I figured once Charlie was dead, I didn't really have to look that hard either. Who else was going to tell? Bobby Knight never really knew for sure what was going on, and I cursed Beth and Charlie's wife so they'd never tell."

Gray was nearly to his station now, the shears on the counter twinkling in the moonlight streaming in from the front windows as if beckoning him closer. "But why use the barbershop to sell your illegal goods?"

"It was the perfect cover." Martin snorted. "People coming and going all the time. Guys hanging around and talking for hours. I only pretended to be friendly with Charlie to have an excuse to come in and hang around all the time. Then there was Beth too, of course…"

The wistful note in Martin's voice caught Gray's attention, and the pieces fell into place at last. "It was you, wasn't it? In the love triangle with Beth and Bobby. You were the other man."

"Except Bobby Knight was nothing compared to me," Martin sneered. "Beth loved me!"

Gray's fingertips brushed the edge of the counter. "Charlie Stevens didn't kill himself, did he? His wife was right, and Eric was about to discover the truth."

Martin let loose another derisive snort. "Eric Naill was too clever for his own good. He knew somehow that Charlie had evidence hidden somewhere. But I'm smarter. I was already tailing him that night. I only used Beth as a ruse. It was Eric I was really watching. So when he came here and broke the back door lock magically, I was right behind him. I killed him because he was too close to the truth. I made only one mistake. I didn't realize the evidence was actually here in the shop. All those years it was empty, who would have thought? But now you've come and ruined everything, and now that you know the truth, I have to kill you, too. I've kept this secret for thirty years. Another thirty should be little problem."

He raised his staff overhead, and bright light exploded from the tip, bouncing off the walls of the salon. Gray ducked to avoid a stray bolt and extended his hand toward the shears on the counter, yelling a charm, *"Excaliber Gladuis!"*

Several pairs of scissors flew through the air toward Martin, embedding themselves in his staff with a dull *thwack, thwack, thwack.* Several shot into the wizard's chest.

The glow from the staff faltered, and Gray seized his chance, rushing Martin. The wizard dodged out of the way at the last second and tossed his staff aside, holding his hand out to Gray instead. Hot-blue jets of flame struck Gray in the chest, hurling him backward.

He managed to snag a can of shaving cream from a shelf as he stumbled and pointed it toward his opponent. *"Inaedifico!"*

White foam covered Martin's face and neck, momentarily blinding him.

Gray gestured toward his curling irons. *"Meridium!"*

Grabbing one of the red-hot glowing instruments, Gray charged once more. Martin managed to clear his eyes and seized his staff, bringing it up in front of him like a sword.

They battled and parried, the curling iron sizzling into the wood whenever the weapons touched, but Martin soon knocked the curling iron from Gray's hands. Gray steeled himself for the worst. Martin might be weakened from the scissors still dangling from his chest, but those wounds were superficial at best. They wouldn't hold off his determined opponent for long.

Martin charged, and Gray dropped and rolled to the other side of the shop. Martin was quick. He turned, holding his staff before him. Gray's heart sank. He had no weapon now. He needed some kind of distraction, but —

Squawk! *I got you covered, boss!*

Cosmo flew overhead with a smock and dropped it over Martin's head, giving Gray an opportunity to seize another weapon. He took the first thing he saw — a straight razor. *"Dolorzio!"*

The razor flew toward Martin just as he broke free of the cape. Martin's eyes widened. He darted to the side, his ponytail flying out behind him. He narrowly avoided being sliced. His ponytail, however, was not so lucky. The blade sliced clean through it, severing his powers.

Silence reigned as the long strands of hair fell to the floor as if in slow motion.

Brimstone purred from beneath his hiding spot under the counter. "Uh oh!"

Martin glared down at his severed ponytail and then at Gray. Cutting off a wizard's hair was no trivial matter. His cheeks flushed, and his eyes glittered with rage. He lunged for Gray, tackling him, anger giving him nearly superhuman strength. Martin tried to land a punch as they rolled on the floor. Martin pinned Gray beneath him and ripped one of the pairs of shears from his chest, raising them high above his head, his gaze crazy with fury.

Gray squeezed his eyes shut, teeth gritted against the stabbing agony to come.

Pop!

The sound reverberated through the salon, and Gray frowned as he felt Martin's weight topple off of him. He slit one eye to see his opponent stiff and motionless on the floor, Luigi standing over him, a thin, knobby wizard's staff still smoking in his hands.

Luigi gave the staff a self-satisfied smile and held out a hand to help Gray to his feet. "Don't figure the Wizard Tribunal will like what I did much, but looks like I still got what it takes, eh?"

Gray stood and brushed himself off. "Is he dead?"

"Nah." Luigi circled Martin on the floor, his boots thudding. For some reason, the guy seemed taller now with the staff still in his hands. "He's not dead. Still breathing. Just out cold."

Even Brimstone seemed impressed with Luigi as he sniffed around his feet.

"How did you even know to show up here?" Gray asked, still trying to collect himself.

Luigi kicked Martin's ponytail out of the way. "I followed him from O'Hara's earlier, guessing what might be about to go down. Your saying he was snooping around the back door is what tipped me off. No reason for him to come back here. Never liked the guy anyway. Pompous ass."

Gray took a deep breath to calm his frayed nerves. "I

saw you earlier, from O'Hara's. We were there to talk to Beth again. But I thought you were working with him."

"Never. It took me a bit to figure it out, but once I realized he was only investigating you to cover his own tracks, I knew what I had to do." Luigi shrugged. "I've had my suspicions about him for a while now."

Brimstone took a seat near the mismatched tiles. "Don't forget about the papers in here. My guess is they explain everything."

Using the key, Gray unlocked the opening and removed the scroll. He and Luigi looked it over together. Sure enough, it was a wealth of information on the old scandal — photos, receipts, even a handwritten account from Charlie Stevens about what he suspected was going on.

"Looks like Martin was the one dealing in toad warts back then. Poor Charlie just stumbled upon his illegal enterprise and paid the ultimate price for it." Luigi shook his head. "That won't go down well with the tribunal."

"Neither will the fact that he cursed Beth Wilkins and Mrs. Stevens to keep them from remembering the truth," Gray said. "Martin admitted it all."

"Right." Luigi set the staff aside and pulled out his cell phone. "For now, let's get rid of the magic and call Owen. We both heard Martin confess to killing Eric, yes?"

Gray nodded.

"Good. I don't think we'll get any argument from

Martin once he comes to. Being incarcerated in human jail will be much more pleasant than what the Council of Wizards would do to him after the tribunal passes judgment. To avoid that, I'm sure he'll confess and surrender to Owen."

CHAPTER 25

Gray closed up Shear Magic late a few nights later. His first day back in business had been busy. He'd moved up some of his appointments, and with the backlog to catch up on, he'd pulled double duty. Nearly everyone who'd come in had demanded the "Mrs. Newcastle" cut. It had been weird and hard without his special golden shears, but Starla had been right. He'd done just fine on his own.

Whistling to himself, he walked the short distance to the juice bar, Cosmo preening and cawing on his shoulder. The early-spring night still held a bit of a chill, but nothing a New Englander couldn't handle. He zipped up his hoodie and shoved his hands into his pockets.

As he crossed the street, a figure stepped out from the alley ahead, and Gray froze. Cosmo's claws dug into his skin, and the cockatoo's bright-yellow comb rose from the top of his head — never a good sign. The ominous shadow moved closer to stand beneath a nearby street-light, and Gray's eyes widened with surprise.

Bobby Knight.

Huh. It was quite a risk for the guy to come to the North Side, especially given what had just happened with Martin Ellsworth and the whole Charlie Stevens case. Bobby seemed oddly placating, though, holding his hands out in front of him in the universal sign of surrender, his dark-violet gaze darting around nervously.

"Um, hey," Bobby said, standing a foot or so from Gray. "I, uh, came to say thank you. I tried to make it as easy as possible for Starla to find that key."

Gray frowned and glanced around then directed Bobby back into the alley for privacy. He wasn't sure how he felt about knowing Starla's uncle had not only spied on them but had interceded in Gray's investigation. "So you knew about our meetings?"

"I had to," Bobby said, giving a slight nod. "There was too much on the line, and I knew I couldn't take the evidence to anyone myself because it would look too suspicious. Charlie gave me that key thirty years ago and told me to protect it. I had no idea what it was for. I only knew I had made a promise, and I needed to keep it." He gave a sad little chuckle. "Despite being from opposite sides of town, Charlie and I were friends. Back then, it wasn't such a big deal. Then things went south and Charlie got killed, and I got scared."

"I'm sorry."

"Not your fault." Bobby shrugged. "I'm thankful you cleared it all up for all of us. It's like a truce or something. You did me a favor, man, and I won't forget it. Here. I brought you a token of my appreciation."

'Oh, well, I —" Gray started, but Bobby held up a hand, cutting him off, and thrust a small brown package at him. The postmark on the box was from Switzerland.

Heart in his throat, Gray opened it slowly to find a shiny new pair of magical golden shears inside. At the bottom was a note from the old wizard: "To a true and faithful artist. Sorry it took so long. I had to forge a new pair."

Stunned, Gray looked up at Bobby. "But how…"

"Gustav is an old friend. He tried to text you back, but he's not good with technology, so he asked me to deliver them to you. I'm only sorry I couldn't bring them sooner, but you know — with the whole feud situation and all."

"Wow!" Gray carefully closed the box and slipped it into the front pocket of his hoodie. "I don't know what to say except thank you."

"You're welcome." Voices echoed from down the street, getting closer, and Bobby stepped back into the shadows. "I need to go. Shouldn't be here at all. Just wanted to say my piece and give you the package. See you around, Quinn." Bobby disappeared as fast as he'd arrived, leaving Gray to stare after him, slightly befuddled.

He made his way to the juice bar, still a bit dazed, and ordered his favorite Tahitian Sunrise before taking a seat at the table where everyone was already gathered. DeeDee related how Martin Ellsworth had confessed right away and was being held at the county jail until his trial.

"It's open and shut, really," she said, sitting back in her chair, Caine's arm around her shoulder. "Good thing, too, after how long the old case went unsolved."

"Congrats on nabbing a murderer, cuz," Ember said from across the table, grinning. "Must feel good doing your part to keep Silver Hollow safe."

Gray cleared his throat, embarrassed heat prickling up his neck. He didn't mind the attention, but playing the local hero was a new role for him after all the recent events. "Thanks. It wasn't me, though. Luigi was the real star of the evening. He knocked Ellsworth out for good."

"Stop being so modest," Luigi said, delivering a complimentary pizza to their table. "You weakened him before I got there, with the scissors and hacking off his ponytail. Made my job a lot easier."

"How about we call it a group effort?" Gray asked, smiling at all the people at the table. "We all played a role."

"Agreed." Luigi pulled up a chair as everyone dug into the pizza. The delicious smells of sausage and roasted garlic filled the air. "At least I'm in better standing with the tribunal now. Don't plan to go back to wizarding full time yet, though. I like making pizza too much."

"How does the tribunal feel about your choice?" Raine asked around a mouthful of crust.

"They're good with it, surprisingly," Luigi said. "Seems maybe they're loosening up a bit. Like some of the old things that were taboo might not be so bad in the future." He glanced at Gray, catching his eye. "Take fraternizing with South Side witches. The familiars already mingle without repercussions, so why not us?"

As if to prove the point, Brimstone strolled by with Starla's cat, Elvira, the orange-striped tabby.

Apparently Gray wasn't the only one to fall under a Knight spell. He gave a short laugh and sipped his drink, his gaze drifting across the town square as the others chattered away. Through the shadows of a doorway, a hooded figure emerged. He looked harder in the shadows to see Starla. Awareness zinged through him, and his throat constricted with yearning. She stepped beneath the orange glow of a streetlight, and their eyes locked. The air between them stretched taut, electrified, before she gave a sad, wistful wave and then turned and walked away, breaking the connection. He gripped the cold metal arms of his chair to keep from rushing after her. Someday he might have the opportunity again, but not tonight. There were too many obstacles still in their path.

Dex trotted up to the table and dropped a kiss on the

top of Issy's head. "Sorry I'm late. I had to drop Stan off at the airport."

"He left town?" Gray asked.

Dex slid an empty chair from a neighboring table between Raine and Issy. "Yep. Headed back to the home office, thankfully."

Ember wiggled her eyebrows. "I thought maybe Ursula would talk him into staying."

"Let's hope not," DeeDee said. "She's a great distraction when he's here, but does anyone really want him hanging around?"

"Not me." Dex stole a sip of Issy's drink, and she swatted his hand away. "He's a pain in the butt, and it's hard trying to throw him off track when he thinks he's onto a paranormal."

"He was pretty distracted this time. I have to hand it to Ursula," DeeDee admitted.

"Yeah, well, I think we're all better off without Stan Judge in town." Raine slurped the last of her Calypso Crush.

"Agreed," Issy, Ember, Gray, and Dex said in unison.

Tim Stevens and his mother stopped by their table.

"Thanks again for all the hard work you did on my dad's case," Tim said. "Not sure how you did it, but you got Martin to confess to the murder. Dad didn't kill himself, just like Mom always said."

"Yes, thank you all." Mrs. Stevens was much improved now, normal and no longer babbling. "This is the first time I've been out in I can't remember how long."

"Enjoy," Gray said, raising his glass in a toast to her.

They went to the counter to order drinks, and Issy leaned closer to Gray.

"Luigi told me that Martin had to lift all of his curses as part of his punishment," she said, "including the one on Beth Wilkins."

Beth stopped at their table to chat with Raine and thank her for the plant. She looked better, more like her old self. Gray couldn't help wondering if she and Bobby Knight might have a second chance at romance. Technically it was still forbidden, but if things were loosening up, as Luigi had said, then who knew? After all, the guy knew Gustav and had given Gray his precious golden shears. He couldn't be all bad.

The table raised their glasses in another toast, this time to Luigi and Gray. "To catching a killer."

"Cheers!" Gray clinked glasses with all of them, then sat back and fed Cosmo a chunk of pineapple. The stress of the past week evaporated as he looked around the table. He was with family and friends. His business was booming despite what had happened, and he'd been successful even without the golden shears — though now he had a replacement pair.

Everything was perfect. Well, *nearly* perfect. His gaze drifted across the town square to the doorway he'd seen

Starla standing in moments ago. She was gone, and Gray didn't know when — or if — he'd see her again.

Laughter forced his attention back to his table, and a burst of contentment replaced the longing in his heart. Martin Ellsworth had thought he'd gotten away with murder twice, but because of Gray's efforts, he'd been caught. Not only would he pay for his crimes, but the Stevens family now knew the truth about Charlie's death, and Beth and Mrs. Stevens had their memories back. Gray felt a rush of pride for his part in bringing Martin Ellsworth to justice.

He really couldn't complain. He had plenty of people who cared about him, and now that Eric Naill's killer had been caught, he was safe from the wrath of the Wizard Council, the Silver Hollow Police, and the FBPI. And that was all he needed — for now.

****

Sign up for my VIP reader list and I'll send you a free copy of my award winning paranormal cozy mystery Dead Wrong:
https://silverhollow.gr8.com/

Join my Facebook Readers group and get special content and the inside scoop on my books:
https://www.facebook.com/groups/ldobbsreaders

More Books in the Silver Hollow Series:
A Spell of Trouble (Book 1)
Spell Disaster (Book 2)
Nothing To Croak About (Book 3)
Cry Wolf (Book 4)

If you want to receive a text message on your cell phone for new releases, text COZYMYSTERY to 88202 (sorry, this only works for US cell phones!)

Silver Hollow

Paranormal Cozy Mystery Series

***

A Spell of Trouble (Book 1)

Spell Disaster (Book 2)

Nothing to Croak About (Book 3)

Cry Wolf (Book 4)

Shear Magic (Book 5)

Mooseamuck Island

Cozy Mystery Series

* * *

A Zen For Murder

A Crabby Killer

A Treacherous Treasure

Blackmoore Sisters

Cozy Mystery Series

* * *

Dead Wrong

Dead & Buried

Dead Tide

Buried Secrets

Deadly Intentions

A Grave Mistake

Spell Found

Fatal Fortune

Lexy Baker

Cozy Mystery Series

* * *

Lexy Baker Cozy Mystery Series Boxed Set Vol 1 (Books 1-4)

Or buy the books separately:

Killer Cupcakes

Dying For Danish

Murder, Money and Marzipan

3 Bodies and a Biscotti

Brownies, Bodies & Bad Guys

Bake, Battle & Roll

Wedded Blintz

Scones, Skulls & Scams

Ice Cream Murder

Mummified Meringues

Brutal Brulee (Novella)

No Scone Unturned

Cream Puff Killer

Never Say Pie

Lady Katherine Regency Mysteries

***

An Invitation to Murder (Book 1)

The Baffling Burglaries of Bath (Book 2)

Murder at the Ice Ball (Book 3)

A Murderous Affair (Book 4)

Hazel Martin Historical Mystery Series

***

Murder at Lowry House (book 1)

Murder by Misunderstanding (book 2)

Sam Mason Mysteries

(As L. A. Dobbs)

***

Telling Lies (Book 1)

Keeping Secrets (Book 2)

Exposing Truths (Book 3)

Betraying Trust (Book 4)

Killing Dreams (Book 5)

Romantic Comedy

***

Corporate Chaos Series

In Over Her Head (book 1)

Can't Stand the Heat (book 2)

What Goes Around Comes Around (book 3)

Careful What You Wish For (4)

Contemporary Romance

***

Reluctant Romance

Sweet Romance (Written As Annie Dobbs)

Firefly Inn Series

***

Another Chance (Book 1)

Tempting the Rival

Charming the Spy

Pursuing the Traitor

Captivating the Captain

The Unexpected Series:

An Unexpected Proposal

An Unexpected Passion

Dobbs Fancytales:

Dobbs Fancytales Boxed Set Collection

———

Western Historical Romance

* * *

Goldwater Creek Mail Order Brides:

Faith

American Mail Order Brides Series:

Chevonne: Bride of Oklahoma

————————

Magical Romance with a Touch of Mystery

* * *

Something Magical

Curiously Enchanted

http://facebook.com/leighanndobbsbooks

Join her VIP readers group on Facebook:

https://www.facebook.com/groups/ldobbsreaders/

www.ingramcontent.com/pod-product-compliance
Lightning Source LLC
Chambersburg PA
CBHW070311190726
48291CB00012B/1078